and the caregiving heart of the world

Verity Jenkins

Shambhala
&
The Caregiving Heart of the World

"Again, the Kingdom of Heaven is like a merchant on the lookout for choice pearls. When he discovered a pearl of great value, he sold everything he owned and bought it!

Matthew 13:45-46

FORWARD

This series arose from a single moment of inspiration; a five year old opened up her hand and told me she was going to love a very dried bee back to life. In this novel, Shambhala and the Caregiving Heart of the World, I've returned directly to that theme. Little did I know when I started writing this series, that years later, my own Mother with Alzheimer's Dementia would need to be loved back to life. And that's what I did while writing this novel - and for many years beyond that.

I see Ray as being more than just a character in a story, I see Ray as an aspect of all of us.

I have written this story as a love letter to empathetic caregiver in you. May we care for each other and still be adventurous, storytelling, world-changing tricksters.

It's my hope that this story will inspire you to accompany a loved one home.

For all ages - fifteen to one-hundred and fifteen.

Hope you enjoy,

Verity Jenkins

Whitestone Ontario

Dec 2022

COPYRIGHT

This is a work of magical realism. I have woven many biological, ecological, geological and geopolitical facts together with some actual people and historical events. However Ray and the narrative within which I have placed these facts are entirely a work of fiction.

We were designed to learn about the world around us from within an emotionally compelling story. This is Narrative Education. Learning within the context of a story can increase memory and retention by 22x according to Jerome Bruner the author of the *Narrative Construction of Reality* and *Actual Minds, Possible Worlds*.

www.verityjenkins.com

Table of Contents: Shambhala

Book 3

Shambhala

&

The Caregiving Heart of the World

Verity Jenkins

CHAPTER ONE
THE CALL TO ADVENTURE

Earthly Dilemmas

On the last day of school before the summer holidays, I thought about getting a job. It's a Catch 22: if you HAVE a summer job, you can afford to go on adventures, but of course you've got NO REAL TIME. If you DON'T HAVE a summer job, then you've got lots of time but NO MONEY. And not to mention that around Mt. Albert the pickings are pretty slim.

But as usual, Harvey's and the local Foodland are hiring. They're employers of last resort for students who didn't plan their summer employment. Which was me, so I dropped my resumé off at both places the next day. Harvey's gave me a call back, and, following a brief interview, I was on the "team."

On my first day, a middle-aged, balding man asked, "What's your favourite hamburger here?"

I said, "I don't eat meat."

(Which is technically not true; I eat small fish and call myself a loveatarian--and here's a secret: I have tried the Jr. Deluxe, but it hardly counts, as the patty is the size of a postage stamp.)

Then he asked me, "Why are you working here?"

I decided his question deserved a truthful answer, so I said, "It's the only place around that gave me a call back."

"I'm sorry to hear that," he replied. "You deserve better."

Okay, if it had ended right there, everything would have been fine and good. But was my supervisor not overhearing everything! From the shocked look on her face combined with an open mouth, I surmised that the best defence was possibly a good offence.

So right away I said, "Why were you listening in on a private conversation?"

"First of all," she replied, "it's not a private conversation--you're at work, and this is your training day!"

I had to admit she had a point there, but I remembered a quote from Gandhi, "*Stand up and be the change.*"

So I said, "A cow chewing contentedly in a rolling meadow is a beautiful thing, the sound of a lark, the gurgle of a brook, poplars rustling, un-genetically modified wheat blowing in the wind, horses galloping at sunset on a ridge, ripening tomatoes on a vine, my grandmother, my pet meerkat, monarchs migrating, the taste of honey--almost anything in nature. But what is NOT a beautiful thing is HARVEY'S! Harvey's is NOT one of those Beautiful Things!"

Well, everyone had stopped moving. My supervisor's jaw was on the floor, and she was white as a sheet. It was like time stopped. I looked around and saw some worried faces and so hesitantly I added, "But the Chocolate Frosty is--almost--a beautiful thing."

Then I heard a sharp clap. I was sure that a moment later I was going to feel a whack from behind. You just cannot get away with that in the Temple of Beef. Then there was another clap: it was the middle-aged man, and then a few others sprinkled throughout the restaurant began clapping.

I realized it was not going to get any better than this, so I chose my moment and said, "I Quit!" At least there was a sense of theatre.

I could try Foodland, but I think I lost the job at Harvey's because I don't really want a job this summer. Something's nagging on my mind and it has to do with Grandsy.

Grandsy is eighty-five, but do not be deceived by numbers. She's rarely eighty-five--she can be whatever age she likes; mostly during the summer, she's whatever age I am. But guess why I'm really in a funk? During exam week, I went to visit Grandsy, who lives with my uncle and his family in Toronto, and she did not get up out of bed. She always gets out of bed when I come to see her, and yet the last two times I visited, she said she was too tired. Sure, her eyes lit up for a few moments in that old way, but then they clouded over again and she lay her head on the pillow and said she was too tired to go out for food.

Too tired to go out for food! That's never happened before. And although I said, "Of course, Grandsy," I returned to the living room and quietly cried on the couch.

In one of her cupboards Grandsy kept a number of nature poems that she'd written after our walks together. While I was looking for them, I noticed a lidded copper soufflé pan that looked out of place. Out of idle curiosity, I pressed the small lever on the handle, and the lid opened. There was a note written on a bank withdrawal slip--Grandsy had collected a lifetime supply.

Whichever of my very Dearest Family wants this--or wants to discard it!
I send you my Love, And remember every day is a <u>passing</u> day of your life, & it is

very precious.

Whoever you are with, make moments with them <u>very</u> special.
It is not in our power to measure that length of opportunity. It does good to your soul, enhances your life--and there will be no regrets.
Ever Loving Mum xoxo

She had dated it on the outside. It had been written only a few days ago! I grabbed the envelope and ran outside to get some air. A few minutes later, I found myself in one of the parks Grandsy and I often walked to. Almost immediately a bunny jumped across my path, and then I heard a cardinal singing and saw a streak of red flash by. Grandsy's nickname was Betty Bunny, and cardinals were her very favourite birds. I felt like Grandsy was deciding to leave soon, but that nature was giving me a sign that there was a way to bring Grandsy back to life.

When Mum returned from her job at the Chaise Lounge (home of the Lounge Chair!), I told her about how Grandsy was so despondent. That's when Mum dropped the bomb.

"Dear, it could be that Grandsy has Alzheimer's/dementia. I don't want you to miss out--how do you want to spend the summer?"

I was honestly confused. I could try getting a job at Foodland this year, but what about Grandsy? I can hardly believe it--last summer she was so full of life.

And it seems like everyone else has a summer filled with stuff to do. But for me, Mt. Albert is the black hole of activity. The farmers farm, the bankers count money, the commuters commute to their little boxes in the sky--from nine to five. The tellers tell, the writers spell, the introverts dwell, preachers preach where the sinners go. The bakers bake, the addicts shake, the romantics ache, while pleasure-seekers jump into lakes.

And what do the elderly with Alzheimer's do? THEY FORGET.

NO, I will not let Grandsy forget . . . just go quietly into this dark night! It's not for nothing that Fa taught me how to seek knowledge and answers in the form of a Sacred Quest. Fa said that, "Real knowledge is hidden from those who just click with their fingers; real knowledge comes in the form of the Quest." I would go on a Quest to find a way to bring Grandsy back to life!

Yet all experience is an arch wherethro'
Gleams that untravell'd world whose margin fades
Forever and forever when I move

Fa disappeared West of West four years ago. I haven't given up on him, though I think Mum has. We've had no word of him; officially he's listed as a missing person, and the leads have gone cold. I have the opposite problem to the police and the RCMP: I have so many clues that they have, not surprisingly, stopped listening to me. So no one is looking for Fa except me. There is an advantage to this, as everywhere that Fa went in a lifetime of adventure is a possible place for me to find clues to his whereabouts. And although Mum won't talk directly about him, she has a soft spot for my needing to find Fa. Did I mention Mum is risk averse?--just the opposite of Fa--so the only way I have been able to go on quests thus far is to exploit this soft spot and play the "Fa card." I know it sounds deceptive, and last summer it almost backfired, but saving Grandsy is part of the greater good that I'm serving. So I think this justifies a bit of deception.

Also, I'm impatient by nature, and it's easy to convince myself that a certain course of action will lead to where I want to go. But my previous quests have taught me that impatience is actually the longer route; and Mum has helped me become aware that my impulsive nature often gets me into significant trouble. So I have promised Mum and myself that I'd try to be less impulsive. I guess this is my first chance to try this strategy, because although I'm really longing for an adventure, most of all I want the Quest to succeed--I want to help find a way for Grandsy to reengage with life.

So I'm going to renounce the direct route and take the butterfly way. Right away I could hear Fa's voice saying, "Go to the rivers and mountains, these are your teachers. They will always help you with your next steps." This was the only advice he gave that he himself always followed, so at least I knew this was to be my first step.

Meeting the River-Keeper

The land becomes large, alive like an animal; it humbles him in a way he cannot pronounce. It is not that the land is simply beautiful but that it is powerful. Its power derives from the tension between its obvious beauty and its capacity to take life. Its power flows into the mind from a realization of how darkness and light are bound together within it, and the feeling that this is the floor of creation.
Barry Lopez--Arctic Dreams

When Mum returned home, I ran toward her and said, "This weekend, let's go kayaking at the Minden Whitewater preserve!"

"Okay," she responded. "I'll have to get out of a shift but I can call in a favour. Why all of a sudden the Minden Whitewater preserve?"

Do not reveal the nature of your Quest too soon, Fa would advise. So a little misdirection was required. "It's going to be a hot weekend, and I thought we could camp by the river and both cool off."

"You know how dangerous that river is, Ray."

"Yes, Mum, I know. People are swept away all the time. You hardly have a chance to wave goodbye to them."

"Ray, I'm not going unless you take the Gull River seriously."

"Don't forget all the hot kayakers, Mum. Remember that one last year with that big, sexy beard?"

"Ray, don't try to distract me. Promise me you'll take the river seriously."

"Mum, just look at my face--look how serious I am."

I could hardly wait for Friday afternoon when Mum's shift ended. I had the car packed and ready to go when she arrived home. While pulling out of the driveway, Mum went through the list . . .

"A tent each."

"Check."

"Sleeping bags and mattresses."

"Check."

"Swimsuits and not my pink one."

Here was a tricky one. Mum was nearly six feet tall and she was a head-turner, especially in her skimpy pink bathing suit. What I needed was for Mum to be distracted and not watching me at every turn. The pink bathing suit could do this for me.

"Check." I'd have to pay for this one later.

"Vegetables."

"I brought food."

"What kind of food."

"Stuff from Coffeetime."

"Coffeetime! That's not food--that's pure sugar and cheap fats."

"I got a spinach pie for a snack tonight, hot water for tea in a thermos, and an apple fritter for tomorrow morning. After that, we can go shopping in Minden and buy all the vegetables you want . . . Check?"

"Check," Mum said with a resigned groan.

Soon we were on Highway 48 sailing northward, riding over the height of land and then down curving under Lake Simcoe, across to Highway 12, from there zigzagging across to Highway 35. The best of Southern Ontario: east of the Muskokas and north of Lindsay, it's Hicksville all the way. Lake after gleaming lake, tall pines, small cottages, marinas, Kawartha ice cream; an endless string of postcards for rustic.

We arrived at the preserve just before dusk and we got a campsite along the river. Before you begin to imagine an idyllic stretch of river, picture this flowing right by your tent: huge standing waves called haystacks, pillows, holes, eddies, sieves, and hydraulics of every kind--right up to Class V, which is defined as, "Large waves, continuous rapids, large rocks and hazards, maybe a big drop. Often characterized by "must make" moves. Failure to execute a specific manoeuvre at any point may result in serious injury or death."

When you stand beside it, you are literally one inch away from the Reaper. It rages, it rips and it roars right by you; one sudden surge or a simple misstep, and it will pull you down into its watery grasp so fast that you might not even catch one breath. The men and women who play in this river are not kayakers so much as wizards and ballerinas. They feel the call of the thundering rapids in their racing hearts. In their tiny "play" boats, they swirl, plummet, pirouette, leap, and roll. They are part salmon and part butterfly; they are twigs that can be snapped in an instant.

Our tent was set up, and during the twilight, I stood mesmerized by the patterns in the current and the primordial boom of water against boulders. Then, flying out of the mist, a lone kayaker emerged. He somehow spotted me, caught an eddy, and swung in close to where I was standing. He paused for an aeon. I noticed a full beard on a beautiful face. He was completely calm, his eyes like pools in a forest. I fell in and I felt so clearly that he was untamed. The wildness ran through us like a current. He took one stroke backwards, spun, dropped, and was swept away.

His art was knowing the river, his boat, and his own abilities so well that he could play in its presence and power. Had he tamed the river? I didn't think so. I wondered: has the river been his teacher? I fell asleep imagining that kind of aliveness . . .

I awoke at dawn to intense birdsong; the river draws all sorts of birds to it, and, as Fa would say, "The dawn choir is my alarm clock." I lay there and watched the shadows of leaves dancing across my tent. I thought I might as well pray for a clue, a message for my Quest. Maybe I should pray to the river?

"Dear River" . . . no, that's so formal.

"River that is the great lifeblood of this vast living goddess that I am a part of. River that we have used for travel and transportation, that we have dumped our garbage into, that we have channelled and dammed and drained and desecrated and abused in every way possible--and yet in this place and other places parts of you still run wild and pure and free. Teach me what I need to know and help me fulfill my Quest."

I felt I needed some markings on my body, and of course I'd brought our henna kit. So I went over to Mum's small tent. She was not there, so I grabbed the henna and apple fritters, put on my bathing suit, and went down to the river. Mum was sitting on a rock cradling her coffee mug in her hands; the pink bathing suit seemed incongruous with the setting.

"You look great in pink, Mum."

"I looked in my travel bag this morning, and the only things in there were this bathing suit and a bunch of T-shirts. You call that packing? And I specifically asked you NOT to bring my pink bathing suit."

"It's not pink, Mum, it's fuchsia. And you said to pack light."

"I know you're up to something, Ray. I just wish you'd be more straightforward."

"Let's just enjoy ourselves, Mum. We have so little time together these days."

"If I get eaten alive by the bugs, then you'll be hearing about this again."

"Okay, I've brought some henna. Let's have fun like we have at festivals and paint each other with sea dragons, fish, and watery symbols."

"Okay," Mum replied, and I could see that some of her energy was coming back, as she loved using her body to draw attention to sacred symbols. We used the hot water from the thermos and the dye and idled our time away in the early morning.

Quietly moving in the small shallows and eddies beside the big river was a fly fisherman. He reminded me of a blue heron in his careful movements. He stopped just upstream of our rock and began to let out his fly-line, flicking his rod back and forth as the line arced farther and farther behind him and over the river, till he dropped his fly into a little pool of calm water protected by a giant cedar that formed an island of exposed roots in the centre of the river. Then I recognized him as the untamed kayaker of last night. My heart raced a bit faster. He reeled the line in without a bite and tried to give us our privacy on the rock, but he was literally stuck between a rock and a hard place. So he had to excuse himself as he went around us.

"You're the kayaker I saw last night."

"Yes, I am," he replied

"What kind of fly are you using?" I asked.

"I'm alternating between a royal coachman and a black gnat."

I knew something of fishing, as Fa had taught me.

"Dry or wet?"

"Dry."

It was working; he was coming over. Then I noticed that Mum, covered in symbols, wearing her pink bathing suit was like one big lure. Oh, no--I could already see my plan backfiring on me.

We introduced ourselves; his name was Liam.

13

Mum asked if he'd caught any so far. He showed us the watery pouch he carried. "I give some away, and the rest I return to the river."

We marvelled for a few moments at their beauty.

"Would you put two back for us?" My Mum asked.

"Surely I'll do that for you," was his reply.

The hook was set.

Once we finished up our henna tattoos we hung about at the water's edge in our own little worlds waiting for them to dry. Before long, an old man ventured along the river's edge; he came over and introduced himself as the River Keeper.

"My name is not important," he said. "Friends just call me River. I know every inch of this river, and you can't dump in a bucket of soapy water without me knowing about it. What's your folk's names?"

Mum introduced herself by her spirit name, "Willow."

"Well then," River said, "I can see we'll be friends."

"I'm Ray."

There was a pause.

"Ray with an 'e' or 'y'?"

"With a 'y.'" Another pause.

I could see that there was something that River was not telling me, something he was holding back. Because Mum was not yet aware of my new Quest, she was not suspicious.

"Keep it pure," winked River as he headed out.

Later, Liam came by to invite both of us out to "play" in the river.

Mum of course immediately said that it was too dangerous.

"I was not thinking of you putting in up here above Whitefish falls, but the outwash from the Otterslide is safe and yet still lots of fun. I teach at Algonquin Outfitters, so I've got access to the boats."

I had no intention of being a third wheel. I'd done that too often.

"You both go ahead. I've got some things to do around camp."

Mum shot me a look. She did not like it when I put her on the spot like that, but I could also see that she did want to go.

"Like what things around camp?" Mum asked.

I was annoyed by the suspicion.

"Things like setting up the hammock."

"Okay, but not too close to the river."

"How about I use that tree?" I pointed to the big cedar tree whose roots formed an island in the middle of the maelstrom.

"Don't be funny, Ray. Liam will tell you how serious a river it is."

"Certainly," Liam replied hesitantly, "the river is no joke and it needs to be respected but it's also playful like your daughter."

He hadn't completely swallowed the hook.

They arranged a meeting time, and things were back on track. I had time to investigate my own suspicions.

First thing I did was go to the Whitewater Ontario office near the park entrance. It turned out that River was there. I asked him if he had time for a walk.

"Could do," he replied, smiling, "if you are the offspring of a remarkable traveller and explorer."

"You do know Fa!" I burst out.

"Sure do."

"Do you know his whereabouts?" I nearly cried out.

"Sorry on that count, dear. Your Fa has always been one of the most unpredictable people on the planet."

I tried to not sound disappointed--after all, this was more than I was hoping for.

"When did you see him last?"

"Let's see . . . it was spring runoff 2014."

"That was just before he disappeared from our lives."

"Well, isn't that interesting."

"How is it interesting?" I was feeling a bit annoyed by his choice of words.

"Interesting because he left something for me to give you."

"What!" I blurted out. "And you didn't think of giving it to me until I just showed up here!"

"Now, settle down, young lady. There's an explanation for everything; just give me time."

"Okay," I replied, "I'm sorry. It's just that I've been missing him badly and looking for him everywhere. What is it that you have for me?"

"I understand, I really do, and I would have given it to you sooner, much sooner, but your Fa gave me instructions to hang onto it--that you would come and get it."

Saying this, he reached down and unfastened a key that was attached to his belt.

"I haven't taken this off since your father gave it to me. I've worn it every day till now."

"Do you know what the key is to?" I nearly shouted out because I was so scared that this would be another mystery.

"Of course I do. It's to a storage locker about twenty minutes away in Carnarvon."

"What's in the storage locker?"

"Damned if I know. Whatever's in there is for you."

"Can you give me a ride there now?"

"I suppose I can. Will your mom be wondering where you are?"

"She's kayaking with Liam so she won't notice."

"Around a big river like this, we don't work on assumptions like that. If you will go tell your mom, I'll meet you at the upper dam in half an hour."

"Okay, I'll be there."

I confess I have uncertainty around what is outright lying and what is simple misdirection. I think the legal system and our language support me in this. I've compiled a short list (thirty-six) words that are synonymous with lying. As you notice at the end of the list, not a few of these words relate to storytelling:

deceit, deception, dishonesty, disinformation, distortions, evasion, fabrication, falsehood, forgery, inaccuracy, misrepresentation, perjury, slander, aspersions, backbiting, calumny, defamation, falsification, falsity, fib, fraudulence, guile, hyperbole, invention, libel, mendacity, misstatement, prevarication, subterfuge, myth, fable, fiction, whopper, tale, tall tale, white lie

Mendacious . . . sounds like a cool middle name. "Ray Mendacious."

It's just that I'm following a slightly more complicated route in getting to the truth.

So as you might guess I prevaricated in telling Mum that I was going to the storage locker. Why? you might ask. Because Fa taught me that one of the secrets to questing is that you must discover the quest inside the quest. On the outer layer is your *Mundane Quest*, and the inner layer contains your *Sacred*, or *Secret Quest*. This you do not reveal to anyone except in dire emergencies as a last-ditch resort. You see, Fa maintained that visible and invisible forces will line up against you to prevent your going on your Quest. Basically, you need to trick these *Gatekeepers* into letting you pass. Wittingly or unwittingly these *Gatekeepers* prevent idle questers from entering on the dangerous but true quest for knowledge. So until I know the nature of my *Mundane* and *Secret Quests* . . . Mum's the word.

Instead of asking Mum, I put some native tobacco, that I keep for offerings, in the river and asked the river's permission. Above the roar I could not hear an answer, so I took that as a yes, then headed upstream to the upper dam. River had the good grace not to ask if I'd gotten Mum's permission--there are advantages to being sixteen.

Fa's Secret Message

We drove to Carnarvon in silence, my mind filled with anticipation and wonder at what I might find in that storage locker. Would it provide clues to Fa's disappearance and where he's gone? Would I find a secret treasure? Would it hold information that was hard to bear? I guess it could be any of these things.

River punched in a code, and the gate opened. We drove through a maze of smaller and larger garage doors till we pulled up in front of locker 107. It looked like any other--except that it was on the last row and had an amazing view of the surrounding forest and rocky outcroppings.

Dust had gotten into the lock, and the key was hard to turn. I was scared at what I might find, yet I couldn't walk away.

Finally the padlock clicked open. I unhooked the lock and looked over at River, who was behind me but keeping his distance. He nodded at me. I took a deep breath and pulled up the door. It made a ghastly noise, but all my attention was focused on what was inside. It took a while for my eyes to adjust to the darkness. The locker was quite big inside, and all I could see was a table with one chair in the centre. I slowly walked toward it. On the table there was a letter, a book, and a piece of wood.

I looked back at River; he was standing in the sunlight. He took his hat off and said that he'd be there for however long it took. I sat down in the chair and opened the letter.

My Dearest Ray of Sunlight,

It's no accident that you are sitting here. I do not know what difficulty you are facing or what you care about so deeply that you are undertaking a Sacred Quest. I presume if you are reading this that I have not returned from my last quest. As you well know, "If the return were certain it would be no adventure."

Here's an Air Canada Air Miles card in your name. It has enough points on it to get you around the world a few times. That is, if they are still using that abominable form of travel, the jet plane. Don't fall into the trap of believing you need to get on a plane for an adventure to happen. I'm still ticked off that Pierre Trudeau is credited with something I said when we were out paddling on Meech Lake.

What sets a canoeing expedition apart is that it purifies you more rapidly and inescapably than any other travel. Travel a thousand miles by train and you are a brute; pedal five hundred on a bicycle and you remain basically a bourgeois; paddle a hundred in a canoe and you are already a child of nature.

You were born in the forest as a child of nature. I am leaving you a clue as to a more hidden aspect of your name that you do not yet know. Ray is also hidden in the word VajRAYana. It is an ancient system of mindfulness that migrated 1,200 years ago from India's great University of Nalanda. At that time, the university housed 30,000 students; some of those students left to spread the Dharma to Tibet and Mongolia. Isolated as they were, a unique Tantric form of Buddhism developed in this isolated region of soaring peaks and thunderous rivers. Many of the indigenous Bon Po earth spirits were married to Hindu goddesses to form a mindfulness practice that instead of taking many lifetimes to reach enlightenment--with Vajrayana (tantric) Buddhism you can travel that distance in a single lifetime. It's not without risks, mind you, often misunderstood, and certainly not for the faint of heart. Sacred Quests are at the heart of its teachings.

I have left you a guidebook, *Magic and Mystery in Tibet,* by a friend and fellow traveler, Alexandra David-Neel. It will allow you to see quests differently and penetrate to the core of the Vajrayana's secrets and hidden ways.

Also, as my return is uncertain, I have left you my most precious talisman, my first river tooth. It is a metaphor that I have found keeps giving me deeper insights into myself and the adventure of life.

Finally, do not be concerned for me. I have been knocking at the door of other realms for my entire life and this means that one has opened. This is a cause for celebration.

Life is an adventure or it is nothing at all.

Farewell and good luck on your Quests. I will always be with you.

Your Everloving Fa

p.s. Take care of your Grandsy--she is the *Pearl of Great Price.*

p.p.s. Remember, "You rise by that with which you fall."

I took the river tooth in my hand. It was three inches long and about two wide. Beautiful swirls of woodgrain, polished and imbued with the oil of Fa's skin. It was in the perfect shape of a giant front molar. I had often seen Fa pull it out of some hidden pocket and roll it in his hands and hold it over his heart, but when I asked him the story, he'd always say, "That's for another time."

I folded up the letter, picked up the river tooth, the Air Miles card, and the book. Closed the door on the storage locker. I felt a mix of emotions, anger definitely one of them. There was still no answer! Everything was a clue, one fucking clue after another. Would it be too much for there to be an answer every once in a while?

Maybe, "Here's his body, he fell, he got altitude sickness then pulmonary edema and he died." Talk about lack of closure. I have to do something about this or I'll be spending my twenties in therapy.

By the time I got to where River was standing, I was a mess. River put his arm around me and noticed the river tooth in my hand.

"Ohhh," he crooned, "can I take a look at that? I remember it; it's a perfect specimen."

"You know what a river tooth is?"

"Do I know what a river tooth is? If I don't then my name's not River."

A smile cracked through my messy wet face. "Do you know the story of *this* river tooth?"

The Rivertooth: Dense with Meaning

River took it in his hand and turned it over. "I sure do. This is the first river tooth I ever remember seeing. Your Fa showed it to me many years ago. After seeing it and learning what a river tooth was, I went looking for my own river teeth and I dare say that's how I came to fall in love with Rivers. Now I've got my own collection."

I felt my sense of curiosity returning. "Can you tell me the story of the river tooth?"

"Sure can, let's grab a growler from the Boshkung Brewery across the street and head up to the log chute at the top of Big Hawk Lake Road, and I'll tell the story. How about you grab the beer, and I'll get an apple spice tea and a few sweet things from Tim's and meet you back at the car."

"Okay. Get a Boston Cream for me."

We drove along the picturesque Kenisis River up to the last working log chute in Ontario. The water thundered through a giant wooden channel into a series of waterfalls. We sat in a cedary little nook in the cliffside with swirling whitewater below and spiralling hawks above. River took a swig of local ale and took out what looked like a sabre tooth tiger fang but it was made from wood. He put it beside Fa's smaller but more civilized-looking molar. "Notice how different these are, but they are still both river teeth."

"Where do they come from?" I asked.

"They are only made in the river."

"How does the river make them?"

"See if you can guess."

"Well," I turned them around in my hands. I noticed that both had similar markings where a tooth would attach to the jaw.

"Is this where the branch attaches to the trunk?"

"Yes, that's exactly right. Go on . . ."

"Is it the dense heartwood?"

"No, not exactly, although it does extend into the heartwood. Actually it's a three-dimensional knot. You see them cross-sectioned in boards of lumber. Well the river does not cut through them like a blade. It sculpts them out of the wood like an artist. The movement, grinding, and shear forces are relentless, and it takes decades for the tree to be broken apart by the river and returned to become soil for new trees to grow in. Just a few of those knots stay in and are shaped by the river. Until all that remains are these pitch-hardened and cross-grained river teeth. So dense that if you cut them in half, some of them are more like glass."

"And are they always shaped like teeth?"

"They are teeth that are only limited by your imagination."

"Are they only found in the river?"

"Yes, they can only be shaped by the forces of the river. However, there are also forest-teeth that are created by the much more tame forces of disintegration in the forest, and are also easier to spot and find.

"But enough talk about river teeth. I brought you to this log chute because not far from here is a pristine logjam with trapped driftwood extending back many years. It's also pretty well untouched; so the likelihood of finding a river tooth there is pretty high--though never guaranteed. It takes a way of seeing to notice them. Perhaps I shouldn't, but I'll tell you this: There is a secret to seeing them. For a few years, I looked only for river teeth shaped like human teeth and I found almost nothing . . . until I looked at all that exists within my own psyche: animals, monsters, demons, witches, and all the creatures of my imagination. If you can search your own psyche, you will find them in the river."

"I can hardly wait."

We crossed the dam to the other side of the river, pulled ourselves up, and climbed a series of switchbacks that allowed us to zigzag up the cliff. Then in a small saddle, River instructed me, "Leave trail and climb through a crack in the cliff face. This will take you to a slab that angles down toward the river. Just follow the slope till it takes you to the river. Just beyond this is the logjam; you can't miss it. Take only what you can carry out. I will be waiting for you back up the road at the marina. Don't rush--take as long as you want. If you get lost, just return to the logjam, and I will find you before dark. Clear?"

"What if I get hungry?"

"It's blackberry season. Eat some berries."

"What if a bear gets hungry?"

"Give it your berries."

"No, seriously."

"Seriously, relax. The bear has met many more humans and knows how to behave. It will show you what to do, if you're listening. Most of the time, the bear will get out of your way. If you see a bear, just carefully make your way back to the trail and come and get me."

I climbed through the crack and brought about twenty spiders with me. It took me a while to brush most of them off and peel off the cobwebs. The huge stone slabs angled toward the river and gave me many great views of the foaming water and gorge below. The cliffside sloped down till it came to the logjam River had mentioned. Never in my life seen a collection of such beautiful shapes of wood. As I crawled along large, half-sunken logs exploring the carved shapes of wood, it's hard to explain how my spirit rose up and my imagination soared. I completely lost any sense of time while climbing along those logs. I took to the shore so many big and small pieces; always on the lookout for something that might be a river tooth. Each log I looked at I tried to imagine as a human or monster's tooth. I did find some huge river teeth, too big to carry, but the smaller ones were more elusive.

Farther out on one of the logs, I slipped on the mossy surface and reached out to not be pulled under and grabbed at anything. Then I stood up and realized that it wasn't deep. I waded back to shore against a strong current and then took off my wet clothes to dry them. When I took a closer look at the piece that I had grabbed accidentally, I realized that it was shaped like a fang, and, just like Fa's, at the top were the telltale markings where the branch attaches to the trunk--like molar roots attached to the bone. I now had one of my own! This I called *The Fang*. Then when I looked over the pile of driftwood I'd collected I realized that in that pile was another river tooth. This I called the *Witch's Tooth*. So now I had two river teeth plus Fa's.

I decided that going berry-picking before my clothes were dry was not a good idea. So I found a big, wide cedar tree that curved up out of the riverbank and made an ideal resting spot. I fell asleep lying against the tree. I awoke to a loud crack, and standing a few feet away looking at me with big eyes was a large stag with a good-sized rack of antlers. It stamped its foot and I felt that he was annoyed. Then I looked down. There was a well-worn animal trail going right past my cedar tree to the river. I got down from the tree and moved a few feet away and crouched down. He sniffed the air and remained motionless for a few minutes, then slowly moved down to the water. A few moments later, a doe appeared and then two fawns, both with big white spots. I was surprised to be so close to the deer. As they passed by, the two little fawns came toward me and the doe turned and snorted. The fawns with their gangly legs ran playfully toward their mother.

After their visit, I put my dry clothes back on, and, as it was getting dark, I collected my river teeth and headed back up the cliffside. I was so surprised how quickly it got dark; I could not find the crack in the cliff that would lead me back to the trail. The day sounds turned to night sounds, and I could hear the "whit-a-woos" all around me. I was trapped between two cliffs, one in front that spiralled down to the river, and one behind that rose up like a black tower. The forest was covered in spiderwebs, and these, combined with the mosquitos, drove me to near panic. Once more, I went over to the black, towering cliffs behind me and walked along them feeling with my hands to see if I could find a way through. I came to what appeared to be a large opening with a wind blowing out of it that smelled of animals and old carpets. I clearly heard a bone break then saw a glimmer of firelight. I turned and ran but right away I caught my foot on a rock and over I went.

Next thing I knew, there was an old woman's face above me and a kindly voice saying, let me help you inside. There were lots of warnings going off in my brain, but her voice was reassuring. She was surprisingly strong. Maybe I'd hit my head very hard and she was a bear? I hobbled into the cave propped up by the old lady. The cave was surprisingly large, clean, and well-organized. Herbs were hanging up and inside the smell was a pleasantly aromatic mixture of smoke and herbs.

"Why does the entrance smell of bear?" I asked.

"Because we have an arrangement: The bear has the cave in the winter, and I have it in the summer."

"Like time-share?" I asked.

"Yes, exactly like time-share." She smiled with a full set of teeth.

"Aren't old women in caves supposed to have one tooth?"

"My you are a curious young one. But before we get to more questions, let's take a look at that leg."

I rolled up my pant leg and it was a mess.

"How do you feel?" the old woman asked.

"A bit faint," I admitted, "but not much pain yet."

She poured a few drops of this and that into a cup of water and handed it to me.

"What's this?" I was used to Mum giving me herbal remedies, but this was quite another situation.

"It's a five-flower remedy that I collect and make into a tincture. It's for shock."

"Like Bach's Rescue Remedy?"

"You know it. Yes, almost exactly like Bach's but I add passion flower and hops as a mild relaxant."

"Sounds good." I drank the mixture readily. "What's your name?" I asked. "Mine's Ray."

"Sounds like we're on the same mission. My name is Lenora, which means Shining Light."

We both just smiled and looked into each other's eyes for a quiet few moments. She ended by just nodding her head and then getting to work on a poultice. First she ground the herbs up using a stone mortar and then poured in some boiling water from the hearth. She wrapped the mixture in muslin (gauze) and then wrapped it around my ankle.

"What's in the poultice?"

"Yarrow to stanch the bleeding, comfrey to pull the skin together, and lavender as an antibacterial."

Lenora led me to a comfortable chair by the fire and propped up my leg. I looked up and saw that there was a hole in the ceiling of the cave and I could see stars above. That must have been why the cave was so well ventilated inside.

Lenora gave me some hot tea with more herbs and I drifted off into a wild sleep.

I dreamt that the entire logjam was inside me, and each of the teeth came to life as monsters of every shape and size. And there was Lenora above them outside her cave, with the exact witch's tooth that I had found in the logjam. It felt like she protected the logjam monsters and at the same time she kept them from going beyond simple mischief to harming others. She had tamed and befriended them.

I awoke to Lenora calling my name.

"Is there anyone looking for you?" she asked.

"Oh!" I became wide awake with a start. "Yes, everyone. River and my mum, Willow."

"Well, there's a male voice calling your name and it's not River. I know his voice well."

"Perhaps it's Liam, my mum's new friend."

I could see Lenora's hesitancy, so I said, "If it's Liam, he's a kayaker--a river person."

I could see Lenora's face lighten up and she went out and called his name. Next thing, Liam was there in the cave looking down at my poultice.

"Well," he said. "Fine hiding place you've found here."

"I'm not exactly hiding," I replied.

"Well, I guess we can call off the search party and scuba divers. Your mum was pretty sure you had been swept away and had the entire campground, all the Gull River searching for you. Then when River showed up and said he had taken you to the Kenisis River and you were now lost, the entire search party and diver all drove up to the log chute, and we began searching this area. Now you're drinking tea with your leg up in a cave. If you're not hiding, I advise you go into hiding for a while till things settle down." Liam ended with a big grin, "You are quite the mischief-maker."

"Well, I was injured," I said meekly.

He looked down at the poultice and asked, "Before or after you led River to believe you'd asked for your mum's permission?"

"I think it was after, or perhaps it was before. I'm feeling a bit too lightheaded to answer your questions right now."

"It's not my questions you have to worry about, it's your mother's. I suggest you spend the night here, providing it's okay with this kind person."

"It is best that Ray stay," said Lenora, "especially given that it's nighttime, now."

"Agreed," replied Liam. "I'll be back with your mom before noon tomorrow."

Liam asked about a few of the herbs and remedies; it was obvious that he was somewhat knowledgeable. When he left, Lenora gave him a jar of something she called "bear grease."

"What's that for?" I asked, just as I began drifting back to sleep.

"Sweat lodge," was the last thing I remember hearing.

It was a night of dreams, some so vivid and real that I was able to step outside the dream while dreaming and tell myself that although I was in a dream, it felt just as real, and the emotions were just as strong, as waking life. I'm pretty sure Lenora and her herbs had something to do with this. Just before I awoke, I saw Grandsy and felt an intensity of love that I had only known in waking life. I began to be aware of the smell of coffee and eggs.

"Rise and shine, sunshine."

"That's what my Fa would say in the morning."

"Mine, too."

"What's that smell that I can't make out?"

"Mushrooms."

"What kind?"

"Angel Wings."

"Really?"

"Yes, they actually look like angel wings. Here are some fresh ones. They are pretty easy to recognize and hard to mistake for anything poisonous. I get at least 40 per cent of my food by foraging during the summer."

"What do you do in the winter?"

"I have a home pretty much like everyone else. But living close to nature fills me up. During the winter, I read and prepare for my next summer adventure."

"Don't you get lonely out here by yourself?"

"I know it might sound crazy, but I'm not here by myself. I am surrounded by living things that I come to know by being quiet and observing. I've looked after both my parents right through to the end and also a husband who died a few years ago. I've always loved nature and especially trees and rivers. So in my own way I take care of this river; and the more we take care of things, the more they speak to us. All those that I've taken care of are in my heart, and from there they speak to me; so I'm never lonely and always grateful. It's not that I don't have my moments, but they pass. Now, honey, eat up, enough about me."

I began to eat the most amazing omelet, on par with Grandsy's famous omelets. But I was aware that another question was arising and I knew not to waste the opportunity to ask this wise woman. "My grandmother is eighty-four and she seems to be losing her will to live. She may have dementia or Alzheimer's and is despondent. What should I do?"

"How do you feel about it?" Lenora asked.

"It sucks! But more than that, it's unfair. Grandsy gave her life up for all her family. She was always there and continually helping. She had such a hard life for many years protecting the family from Grandfa's craziness. Now she's got Alzheimer's. How unfair is that!"

"Ray, each of us is an instrument of divine justice. That's our job description. That's where we bring our light."

Just as she said this I let out a big sigh. I knew that I needed time to think about this, that this was important. But just then, Mum and Liam arrived outside the cave.

Right away, Mum took a look at my leg and the poultice and she breathed a sigh of relief. I thought I'd get off easy, but one look from Mum and I knew that she was still upset with me. Despite that, I mustered my courage and introduced Mum and Lenora. Lenora led Mum inside the cave, as Mum was curious--curious and cautious. When they came out, I could see that Mum was more relaxed and they were enjoying each other's company. I'm sure Lenora had some kind words to say about me, as Mum had softened somewhat.

We walked back in silence, interrupted only by Liam making some cheerful remarks about this and that. Each of us responding with only the most basic remarks. It wasn't a hostile silence. Just that both of us were thinking about what we were going to say.

Near the car, Mum broached the subject, "We had two search parties out looking for you at two locations. During the first search, I found that River had given you a key from Fa, and that led us to the second search. Right now, I'm just too curious as to what was in that storage locker to be mad. When I asked River, he said that I had to find out from you. Why would you not let me know where you were going? What was inside that locker? And what's going on with you withholding important information?"

"Mum, that's three questions--"

"Ray, I don't have the patience right now for any evasion."

"Mum--"

"Listen. I know it was one of Fa's techniques to deflect. I heard him use the expression, 'keeping mum' many times. Well, I'm just letting you know that on this occasion it's not going to work."

"Wow, Mum, I can hear you roar."

"Ray, no coaching or praise. Just spill the beans."

"Speaking of spilling the beans, I need a pee break."

"Ray, NO!"

"Mum, just listen to yourself; you're becoming a Nazi. Just let me go to the port-a-potty at the log chute, and I'll spill all."

"Fine, go."

Wow, this was a tight one. I had just a couple of minutes to come up with a plan. The clues were coming to me. "The way down is the way out," "We rise by that with which we fall." Somehow I must go down instead of up. The answer to my Quest lay at the bottom of something. Next, I knew it involved rivers and the river tooth. Instead of following a butterfly or a bee, it was a river tooth. Was it a metaphor I was seeking or something else inside of me? I guess I was not sure yet--perhaps this was the "dire circumstance" Fa spoke of.

"Okay, Mum. I'm going to come clean with you."

"Ray, let me be the judge of that. What did Fa leave you that required a key?"

"A letter, a river tooth, and a book."

"Can I see the letter?"

"Here's the book and the river tooth. I'd prefer to keep the letter to myself, as it's personal."

I handed Mum the river tooth and the book. She accepted them cautiously, turning them both over in her hands. I could see she was thinking.

"Okay, Ray, I can't insist that you let me read the letter Fa wrote to you. But I do hope that one day you'll be willing to share it with me."

"Thanks, Mum, but while we're on the subject the book Fa left, *Magic and Mystery in Tibet*: The contents of the letter do indicate that Fa's last adventure may have been to Nepal or Tibet."

It took a few moments for Mum to take that in. "I guess I shouldn't be all that surprised, as they were some of Fa's favourite places. He was always talking *beyul* this, *beyul* that, some magic land that was outside of the daily responsibilities of life."

"Mum, can we pleeesse go to Tibet this summer? We might find Fa!"

"Ray, you know we're not made of money and that I need to work at the local café this summer."

"But Mum, you always wanted to learn sound healing using the Tibetan Bowls. Wouldn't this be an awesome opportunity? And you know how Fa always talked about how cheap things are in Nepal and Tibet?

"Yes, inexpensive once we got there, but the flights are out of our price range."

"What if I had an Air Miles card with enough air miles on it?"

"That's a huge number of air miles; where'd you get them?"

"I forgot to tell you that an Air Miles card was also in the storage locker."

"What else did you just happen to forget to tell me?"

"Nothing, Mum, I swear."

"Ray, with every truth I discover there's another secret with you. I'm going to have to think about this."

I decided it was best to keep a very low profile the next day. Mum went off kayaking with Liam. I hiked down to Moore Lake and went for a swim, but mostly I hung around the campsite and read. It was great to not be disturbed by any sounds because of the great rush of water. I was reading Alexandra David-Neel's *Magic and Mystery in Tibet* and was interested that it differed from classical Buddhism due to its adoption of the more ancient indigenous teachings of the Bon Po religion of Tibet. I loved that idea--instead of trying to convert the native people of Tibet and Nepal, they integrated the best of both teachings together and created something new. Tantric Buddhism had already borrowed heavily from Hinduism; now it was borrowing from native Tibetan shamans. I looked up the word *syncretism*: it means the combining of different beliefs. I'm going to work this word into my next essay for Mrs. MacFiercesome; it's sure to score a few extra marks. I know what the Latin root "syn" means, because I was diagnosed with synesthesia a few years ago. I have two types, chromesthesia and mirror-neuron synesthesia.

When Mum returned I was just lying down enjoying the sounds of the river, which was triggering a dance of colours in my mind's eye.

"Ray, I have been thinking and I realized that I can't let you go on any significant trips without knowing you're being 100 per cent honest with me. You need to know that your best chance of travelling is by being open and truthful. I've likely contributed to this situation and lack of honesty between us. I realize that you feel the need to skirt around my fears to get my permission to go on adventures or quests. So I'm going to make you a deal. If you tell me the whole truth I will promise that I'll do my best to make your adventures happen and that I won't let my fears stop you. It doesn't mean I'll say yes or need to put safeguards in place. But I will do my best to not come from a place of fear. Agreed?"

Well, Mum had put her cards on the table. It seemed that my best bet was to do the same. "Grandsy's not well; she does not want to get out of bed. It's just not like her. That's the real reason for my Quest."

"Well, why did you not tell me before? I can see that, too, and I'd love to help you with that Quest."

"Well, it's just that I think I'll find the answers to bringing Grandsy back to life, in a cave in the sky"

"What?"

"See, that's why I didn't tell you. These quests don't make logical sense to me either, at the start. I go more by way of intuition. In school, I learned that my ancient limbic brain recognizes a pattern, and, as pieces come together, it either feels right or it doesn't. That's how I navigate on these quests."

"Okay, but I just don't get it--what has a cave to do with Grandsy?"

Well, now I was going out on a limb . . . "Nothing directly, but several clues lead me to think I'm seeking a cave. Fa finished his letter with the Tantric quote: 'We rise by that with which we fall.' So I think perhaps the cave is in the sky."

"This simply does not make sense; it sounds crazy."

"That's why I don't share my quests at this point, they *do* sound crazy. It's a kind of intuitive image or vision. This image of a cave in the sky combines the upper journey with the lower journey and the inner with the outer. That really integrates how both you and Fa want to me travel."

"I have to agree," Mum said, "but how in a practical sense do you know your destination or itinerary?"

"Well, outside of Nepal or Tibet, based on the book Fa left, I don't know any more at this point. This is the "Butterfly Way" and it has steered me well on previous quests. I see what doors open and what synchronicities happen along this path and keep a watch out for my vision or image appearing along the way."

"This approach has nearly gotten you killed on previous quests."

"As Fa would say, 'If the outcome was certain, then it would be no adventure.'"

"Oh, I knew it would not be long before Fa came into this," said Mum.

"Mum, you promised!"

"Okay, Ray. I did promise, and, to keep my end of the bargain, Liam has been planning a kayaking trip to Nepal. He's invited me to be the cook for part of their trip. We can use the Air Miles and go to Nepal together."

"What?" My mouth dropped open.

"Don't seem so surprised; my cooking's not that bad, and I've done a lot of camping."

"You're a good cook, but the Himalayas is not camping in Algonquin park."

"Now who's the killjoy?"

"Yes, but, okay . . . but?"

"Is it that Liam is younger than I am?"

"Maybe--he's closer to my age than he is to your age."

"So what does that mean? Does that mean that you like him?"

"Well, of course I like him; he's pretty likable. But no way, he's not my type."

"At sixteen you already have a type?"

"Let's just forget it, Mum. I'm happy you got invited, and you'll make a great camp cook. That is, if you don't get eaten alive by those massive leeches on the trek in."

"Ray, adventuring is not just you and Fa's domain. I need adventures and encouragement, too. Is it true about the leeches?"

"They're not *that* bad."

"But there are leeches?"

"Yes, but Fa said they are only bad during monsoon season. What river is Liam planning to kayak?"

"I believe he said the Karnali."

"I want to go to the Kali Gandaki."

"Honestly, Ray, sometimes I think I've spoiled you."

"Okay, maybe I could rearrange my butterfly path to include the Karnali."

I Googled the Karnali and immediately liked what I saw. The Karnali is one of the biggest volume rivers. It goes through an extremely narrow canyon, creating one of the longest and highest-rated rapids on earth. It's also got an awesome name. *God's House!*

I was pretty sure that was where Liam was headed. I could feel that the tide had turned and the fates were with me.

The last thing I had to do before going was to get Grandsy's blessing on this Quest. She always had mixed feelings about my going away. She loved adventure and loved that I was going exploring the world and seeking things out; but she was also worried like a mother. Yet she never allowed her worries to get the upper hand or to weigh down my dreams.

Grandsy was in bed and she said in a tired voice, "Give me a few minutes, and I'll get up and we'll have tea in the living room."

It was quite a while later. Grandsy had tried to put on lipstick, and her dress was on crooked. Her rooms were covered in clutter, and there was not an inch of space to even put down our teacups.

I said, "Grandsy, I've noticed you're tired more often and so I'm going on a Quest to find out how to bring you back to life."

"Dearest Ray, I love that you care about your old Grandsy, but more than anything I don't want to be a burden to you or any of my family. I want you to live your lives to the fullest."

"Well I'm going on this Quest because I love you."

"I love you with all my heart. I will love you always and forever, no matter what you do. But since you're going on another dangerous Quest, to keep you safe I'm going to give you my pearl necklace to take with you."

"But Grandsy, never in my life have I seen you without your pearls-- you even shower in them!"

"I have always worn them since I was a young girl, and they have kept me safe and they will do the same for you."

"What do the pearls mean?"

"During my life they have meant many things to me, perhaps like my son's river teeth. But I can't remember much now. Let's see . . . perhaps I might just be able to recall the quote I learned in my convent school . . ."

Even though Grandsy could no longer remember what happened yesterday, she could often quote the Bible and sing many songs . . .

"The kingdom of heaven is like unto a merchant man, seeking goodly pearls
Who, when he had found one pearl of great price,
Went and sold all that he had, and bought it."

"Is that what you did, Grandsy?"

"I guess I did. I own nothing and yet I have all I need. My treasure is my family."

"What is the Pearl of Great Price for you?" I asked.

"You are my Pearl of Great Price," said Grandsy, shuffling toward me in her love and peace slippers, holding her hands out to embrace my face and then planting a big kiss on my cheek--eyes radiating love.

"Grandsy, I will do whatever it takes to bring your energy back so you can feel like your old self."

"That would be marvellous . . ." her voice trailed off, and she crept back to her bed.

CHAPTER TWO
MEETING THE GATEKEEPERS

Queen of the Skies

Thanks to Liam, Fa's air miles, and Mum's new-found adventurousness, we were on our way to Katmandu. At the airport it turned out we were entitled to a $200 upgrade from Economy to First Class. I leapt at the offer, and Liam was ready to go along with it, but Mum refused because of some obviously misguided principle. I had always wanted to see what Business and First Class were like and this was a twenty-hour and thirty-five minute flight. It was a 3,000-dollar upgrade for 200 bucks. It was more like a gift from the gods than a mere upgrade. I maintained it would be sacrilegious to refuse it. Mum and I had the first argument of the trip right in the ticket line. The result was that Liam and I upgraded to First Class, and Mum travelled in Economy.

My instinct was to rub it in. The 747 is called the "Queen of the Skies" for good reason. Especially if you're riding in the bubble, called the top deck. It's more like flying in a super-posh lounge. The seats are luxurious, acres of leg room, hot towels every little while, snacks all the time, fresh t-shirts, slippers, movies. Everything was free. It was so awesome that I was very worried about Mum, seeing how different it was down in "Cargo Class." I went down below to visit with her, and it was much worse than I expected.

The smells in the lower deck were the first thing you noticed, and the density of people was remarkable. The rows were five wide, and there was row upon row with not an attendant in sight. Mum was in the middle of a row, clearly not enjoying herself. The large person to Mum's right was enjoying a constant stream of home-cooked Dim Sum being passed over her by a small woman on Mum's left. A small seating error that no one cared to correct. At that moment they were both crunching on chicken's feet. It was basically every person for themselves, for twenty-plus hours, in an industrial farm-like setting at 60,000 feet. I could not get even get close to Mum, as there was also no leg or elbow room whatsoever.

Mum looked up at me pleadingly, "How's it in business class?"

"Not much better," I replied

"Can I at least come up to stretch my legs and walk around?"

I had checked before coming down, and they were very strict about Business and First-Class passengers only on the upper decks--even though there was lots of room in the lounge.

"Sorry, Mum, I did ask, but they said no way. Looks like you're going to have to stick it out down here. But try to keep in mind it's not much better upstairs."

Well, that was a flat-out lie, but as Fa said, "Hard truths more harm than nice falsehoods do."

I went back upstairs to the lap of luxury and as I was strolling down the ample aisle, I spied a handsome older woman reading a big, well-worn version of Alexandra David-Neel's *Magic and Mystery in Tibet*. Now you tell me this is not providence!

I introduced myself and showed the white-haired woman my pocketbook version of the same title.

She turned it over carefully in her hand as though it was a precious object and it gave me a chance to observe her well-used, leather-bound version.

She introduced herself as Marie-Madeleine Peyronnet.

"Shall I tell you how I came upon my copy of the book and then perhaps you can tell me how yours came to you? First, come and sit down beside me."

Before I relate this to you, so far I have been honest about my falsehoods, and what I'm about to relate to you is so remarkable that you'd be inclined to believe I made it up. If only I possessed such powers of imagination. Everything I'm about to tell you is 100 per cent true. It's gospel, as Fa would say.

"I was a personal assistant--or, as you in North America refer to it, a caregiver--to a most remarkable person, to me the most remarkable person that has ever lived."

Well Marie-Madeleine certainly knew the art of a dramatic opening. I was wriggling with delight at the cusp of what I was sure would be a good story. I could feel the world around me disappearing, and I was entering the world of Marie-Madeleine.

"Just to give you some perspective, the person I'm referring to was born as Eugénie in 1869 in Paris. At two years of age, her father took he to see the last of the communists being executed at Communards' Wall at the *Père-Lachaise* cemetery. It was a barbaric scene that influenced Eugenie for the rest of her life. At your age, she had found a book on the food habits of the saints and was practising their diets and ascetic spiritual practices. At twenty-one, she became a committed Orientalist and was learning Sanskrit and Tibetan and travelling throughout Europe as an opera singer. In 1904, she married and set off on her third trip to India, promising her husband she would return in nineteen months. It was fourteen years before she would return from one of the most remarkable journeys undertaken by any Westerner.

"In that time, Eugenia, now called Alexandra David-Neel, travelled throughout what was then known as the Forbidden Kingdom of Tibet. She lived and studied with the lamas and was to become the first female ordained as a Tibetan Lama. She lived in a cave for five years, adopted a fifteen-year-old Tibetan who was also to become an ordained lama. To the Tibetans, she was one of them. Alexandra could read, write, and speak all the dialects of Tibet. Her adopted son, Yongden, was to go with her on adventure after adventure throughout Asia for the next fifty years until his death when she was eighty-seven."

I was sitting there with my mouth wide open.

"From your expression," Marie-Madeleine continued, "I see you have gathered that I am speaking of none other than the author of the book that you and I are holding, which is precious to us both for various reasons."

I had just "coincidentally" met someone who knew the author of one of the few things Fa left behind for me because we had just happened to be offered an upgrade. Don't tell me life is not stranger than fiction.

"How is it that you entered into her story?"

"In Alexandra's sixty-ninth year, she embarked on a four-year journey throughout China, during which time her husband died in their home just outside of Paris. Instead of returning to Paris, she travelled to a small village in Tibet where she began a five-year retreat. Then, in Alexandra's eighty-seventh year, while on a writing retreat in her home just outside of Paris, her son, Yongden, died suddenly. Alexandra found herself alone in the world. The great adventurer--perhaps the greatest adventurer of both inner and outer worlds--was alone and suffering from articular rheumatism that forced her to walk with crutches. In 1957, she moved into an inexpensive hotel to live. I met her in 1959, a beautiful but fading spirit living alone in difficult circumstances. My heart reached out to her and I became her personal assistant and companion. According to Alexandra David-Neel's official biographer, Jacques Brosse,

[I] watched over her like a daughter over her mother--and sometimes like a mother over her unbearable child--but also like a disciple at the service of her guru.

"Between the years of 1959 and 1969, till the moment of her death at 101, these were the most remarkable years of my life, perhaps the most remarkable years of many lifetimes. During which Alexandra shared with me many of the greatest adventures of her life. Some of these adventures and insights were never written, and no one knows them--but I do, I remember. Now I am returning her ashes together with Yongden's so according to their wishes they are mixed together in the river that flows from the Sacred Mountain into all the world."

The hairs on the back of my neck rose, "What is the name of that river?" I knew it before I asked the question.

"Karnali," replied Marie-Madeleine.

There was a long pause where I nearly blacked out. In my pre-trip research, I had learned that the word Karnali meant "Holy Water from the Sacred Mountain."

"Where had you planned to travel to?" she asked.

"God's House. It's a particular stretch of the Karnali."

"In lots of ways it looks like we're going to the same place," said Marie-Madeleine.

She began writing in her notepad. "I'm writing to a very reputable Sherpa guiding agency based in Katmandu. It's owned by Yongden's son-in-law. I'm writing it on Alexandra David-Neel's personal letterhead. It will no doubt get their attention. In this note I'm authorizing the agency to guide you to a place that perhaps a handful of people on earth know the location of. Millions have heard about it and yet the exact location has been faithfully kept a secret for all these years. Hitler sent an expedition and even they, with their methods, could not locate it; *Lost Horizon* fictionalized it, and the recent series *Lost* was based on it. It's none other than Shambhala or Shangri-La. This was the lifetime quest of Alexandra David-Neel, finding the entranceway to Shambhala."

I was feeling 100 per cent confident in Marie Madeleine until this moment. As soon as she mentioned Hitler and *Lost Horizon*, I knew she was going to say Shambhala. It was the quest of Fa's life to find Shambhala as well, but I'd given up hope that it existed, not to mention that it took Fa away so many times that now I resented even the idea of it. Yet, despite this, there was still just a glimmer of hope that it would yield some clue as to Fa's disappearance.

"You mean to say a travel agency knows the secret to Shambhala?" I said incredulously.

Marie Madeleine replied with a smile, "I know it sounds fantastic; I myself hardly believe it. To see it with my own eyes it why I'm travelling here on what is likely the last trip of my lifetime. But with all I experienced of Alexandra David-Neel, even with her loss of memory in those last years, one of those things that never faded was her vision of Shambhala. She told me the stories of it over and over till I felt like I have been there many times. It simply must exist. And it is not a travel agency, it's a trekking agency--a very special one."

"What do you mean, a very special one?"

"Well, the agency is comprised of monks that are sworn protectors of Shambhala. They have passed their knowledge and secrets on to adepts from generation to generation since the founding of Shambhala."

"Fa told me that Shambhala's Tibetan name is Gyanganj, which means the 'Home of the Immortal Beings.' Is this the same place?"

"Yes, according to Alexandra, Gautama Buddha delivered his highest teaching in South India just before his death. Those who heard this last teaching went off and founded Shambhala to protect those teachings for all time. Among them was King Suchandra, who became the first king of Gyanganj."

"Fa said those teachings were the pinnacle of Buddhism and were called the Kalachakra--meaning 'Wheel of Time.'"

"Your Fa taught you well, and it is clear to me that we were destined to meet." Marie Madeleine handed me the note and also a cryptic map she had drawn on the back of an envelope. The only word I could decipher on it was "Shambhala Trekking Agency."

"That's subtle," I said.

"Sometimes the best approach is to hide things in plain sight. Go to this agency in Katmandu and give them this letter; it contains all they need to know."

I glanced at the note. It did not refer to Shambhala but to "the Palace of the Three Veils." "What's 'the Palace of the Three Veils'?" I asked.

"It's the only gateway to and from Shambhala. Goodbye and good luck, Ray. Perhaps we will see each other next in Shambhala!"

I returned to my seat across from Liam. He opened one eye and went back to sleep. I reclined my chair, put my slippers on, and donned the eye mask. What could be better? I was riding the *River of God* to the *Land of the Immortals*, where I would learn the secrets of the *Wheel of Time*. My Quest was falling into place. Perhaps I would find the secret that would bring Grandsy back to life.

Liam's Backstory

The next thing I remembered was being jolted awake by a loud announcement.

"This is your captain speaking. Please fasten your seatbelts. We are encountering turbulence as we cross over the western end of the Himalayas in order to avoid a large storm cell. There are significant anabatic updrafts, as the jet stream has descended and is being deflected up from the summits of the mountains below us."

Liam leaned over toward me, and I noticed he looked surprisingly uneasy for such a calm and collected guy.

"What's wrong, Liam?"

"Those winds the captain mentioned are connected to my sister's death last year."

This was the first time I'd heard about his sister's death. He had not talked about himself at all. Or maybe I was just too absorbed in my own matters . . .

"What happened to your sister?" I asked. "Of course, if you're not ready to talk about it, I understand."

"It's no secret," Liam replied.

"I'm all ears."

"The anabatic winds that the captain spoke of are caused by the sun warming the air around a mountaintop. As a result the cooler air below it rushes toward the warmer air through convection, and this causes a low pressure above the mountaintop. Then more air rushes up the ramp-like slope toward the low pressure, often in the form of a ball accelerating off the top of a peak. In extreme cases, anabatic winds can reach bullet-like speeds and are invisible unless they touch ground or water. My sister was killed in part by the opposite kind of wind, a katabatic wind."

"Okay, Liam," I ventured, "perhaps enough of the meteorology lesson."

"Well, this wind came down from Haleakalā volcano."

I'm always interested in the name of things. I've found that often people and places are true to their names, so I interjected, "What's 'Haleakalā' mean?"

"House of the Sun."

"That makes sense now."

"What, my sister's death?"

"Oh, no," I'd put my foot in it, "not your sister's death. But the katabatic winds being heated by the sun."

"Okay, so now you're more interested in mythology than

36

meteorology."

"I guess I am . . . sorry to interrupt. You were saying the wind came down from Haleakalā."

"Yes, right out of the blue this freak wind came straight down the mountain like a piece of the jet stream breaking off. It picked up speed as it rolled down Haleakalā right into the bay where Heather was windsurfing along the shore break. It snapped her mast and knocked her unconscious, then the breaking waves pulled her under and trapped her on the coral reef. In a few minutes, she was dead; but it took weeks for us to find her.

"I was visiting her for the month, and we went out windsurfing nearly every day. This was the one day I went into town and she headed out by herself. I know it's not my fault, but you can't help wonder what if . . . ?"

I was silent for a few moments, as I had my own "what ifs" to wonder about.

"You were a windsurfer?" I asked.

"Yes. Heather was more committed to the sport and more accomplished than I was. I kayaked and windsurfed. I just love playing in the elements. But after my sister died, it was too much for our mother. I quit windsurfing and concentrated on kayaking. It did not have such negative connections for the family, and I really wanted to at least spare them that."

"Was there a memorable moment during that last visit with Heather?" I asked.

"Funny you should ask that, because something unusual happened just the day before. There were more dolphins in the bay than we'd ever seen. They were riding the waves, often right alongside our boards, clicking at us in the most comradely kind of way. Then for a few minutes they seemed to be warning us away. It was a bizarre change that left us both feeling uneasy. We were about to head in from the ocean to mouth of the bay when we spotted a pod of killer whales heading in our direction. We signalled each other and, with a little anxiety, we headed back toward the shore break. I turned my head and they were still heading in our direction. Next thing I knew, Heather was being lifted up out of the water. She was still on the windsurfer but the board was directly on top of the killer whale's back. A few moments later, the whale submerged, and Heather continued on toward shore. Even at the time, we both felt it was some kind of omen or foreshadowing, but that night we went out drinking, told the story a few times, and shrugged it off. Had I listened to my intuition, I might have stayed with Heather for the next few days or insisted she come hiking with me that day."

"I remember the day Fa left. I keep playing it back over and over;

each time, I change what I said to him at the airport and wonder if that would somehow have brought him back."

"What did you say to him?"

"I wish out of all the things I've said, I could take those back.

"I said to him, with the amount of time he was gone away, he might as well not come back."

"Surely that's a coincidence and has nothing to do with him not coming back."

"Maybe, maybe not."

"I'm sorry," replied Liam.

"I'm sorry for the loss of your sister, Liam."

We both got up out of our seats and embraced in a good long hug.

I fell asleep again and next thing I heard was, "This is your captain again. We are beginning our descent to Kathmandu International Airport. If you look to your right, you will see the upper pyramid of Mount Everest catching the sunlight."

I looked down and saw the peak lit up like it was on fire.

Liam peered at me over this month's *Paddling* magazine. "Just imagine how many have died to reach this remote summit that we so easily fly over."

"Fa said that if you are not enough going up Mount Everest, you won't be enough coming down."

"I agree taking physical risks does not significantly build self-esteem, but it's just one motivation--there are other virtues to adventure."

"Like?"

"The focus and feeling of flow that is like meditation in action . . . Your body being able to do remarkable things with training . . . The managed risk that makes you feel truly alive . . . The presence of the awesome power of nature that you are a part of."

I liked how Liam's face and especially his eyes lit up when he talked about adventure.

"You know, Liam, I agree with you. I think we all need a sense of adventure in any stage of life. Grandsy and I would go into nature, but she never liked the word 'hiking.' If I said we were going hiking, somehow she would not be able to make it. But if I called it a picnic, she'd walk almost anywhere. Each outing was an adventure."

"Sounds like I'd get along with your Grandsy."

"You would, although she'd test you a few times to see what your intentions were."

I thought that would lead him off this line of inquiry and get him talking about himself and Mum. But he didn't take the bait.

"Tell me more about your Grandsy."

I'd planned to keep my Quest a secret, but it was so honest and sincere a question that it took me by surprise.

"There's something wrong with Grandsy. The family is just kind of accepting that this is Grandsy's life stage, and the illness is nature taking its course. But I don't think so. She won't admit it but she's kind of given up. Perhaps it's Fa not returning but it's also a lack of meaning. Her children are too busy with their careers. Her grandchildren are now teenagers and we have our own lives. Everyone checks on how Grandsy's doing, but each of us hardly has time for her outside of asking about her health at the few family get-togethers each year. She's well managed, but I believe she feels irrelevant and she's afraid she'll become a burden."

"How do you know all this? How old are you, anyway?"

"So here's my secret, a very simple secret, 'It is only with the heart that one can see rightly; what is essential is invisible to the eye.'"

"Haven't I read that somewhere before?"

"I do hope so--it's from one of Fa's and my favourite stories, *The Little Prince*, by Saint-Exupery."

"Why are you going on this journey, then, if you can see that Grandsy needs care?"

"I guess I don't believe I can alter the situation by myself."

"Perhaps this is another virtue of adventure--believing in yourself."

"Look down there. The fabled city of Kathmandu," Liam said, pointing to a vast area of small lines and buildings.

"It does not look like any other city from the air; there's no green space, just building after building following narrow streets in no recognizable pattern."

"That's it, there's no place like it!"

The Fabled City

Well, it all rushed by so quickly. The moment we got off our big living room in the sky, we were not in Kansas anymore . . . we were plunked down in the middle of Asia. We struggled around the baggage handling area and eventually found Mum. She looked like she'd been awake for all of the past twenty-one hours. We both enclosed her in a long hug. Liam got our bags and ferried us through the crowds into one of the hundreds of taxis each trying to coax us inside.

On the flight, I'd looked through the Lonely Planet website for Kathmandu, so when the taxi driver asked if we'd like him to recommend a good hotel I said, "No, we've decided on the Kathmandu Guest House, and it should take no more than fifteen minutes to get to from here." The driver turned around and glared at me, but I just sat there smugly. It was good to be travelling again.

When we arrived, we discovered that because we'd not reserved a room in the new wing we were put in the old wing, which was being demolished. I should have read the fine print on their website. Mum was too tired to find another guest house. We collapsed on beds that sagged beyond the limits of the western spine. Thank goodness Mum and I practised yoga.

Liam decided to go and look for food, I decided I was more curious than tired and followed him into the popular Thamel district. We got no more than ten steps from the guest house when a mother cradling a not very alert baby came up to us and begged for money. I gave her a few US dollars that I had, and then she pushed very close to Liam and shoved her baby toward him and said, "Money for baby."

"But I've just given you a lot of money. That was for both of us," I stated.

The woman ignored me and again pushed her baby toward Liam, and so he started to back away, and I followed him. Bizarrely, the woman and baby were in hot pursuit. Liam ducked into Paradise Book House. The owner stood at the door and the woman knew not to follow us. We browsed this great bookshop for a while. I found a book on "Heartmath," but Liam told me it was based on pseudo-science. He said the philosophy was sound but the science was weak. I put it on the maybe pile. The next thing that caught my eye was, *Fearless in Tibet: The Life of the Mystic Terton Sogyal*. He was the teacher of the thirteenth Dalai Lama during the invasion of Tibet and a master at teaching heart-opening practices. Oho, then I found a book that I knew I was going to love: *The Heart of the World: A Journey to Tibet's Lost Paradise* by Ian Baker. This was just the kind of instruction I needed to find hidden places--*beyuls*, as they are called in Tibetan. There were lots of Alexandra David-Neel's books-- in fact, an entire shelf of them: *My Journey to Lhasa: The Classic Story of the Only Western Woman Who Succeeded in Entering the Forbidden City; Immortality and Reincarnation: Wisdom from the Forbidden Journey; Tibetan Tale of Love and Magic;The Superhuman Life of Gesar of Ling; The Power of Nothingness;* and the hard-to-come-by *The Secret Oral Teachings in Tibetan Buddhist Sects.*

I grabbed them all.

Finally, Liam came out with one or two adventure stories of kayakers doing first descents but nothing to match my teetering pile of books.

"You can't travel with all of those books," Liam blurted out.

"I'd prefer to leave my lifejacket behind than any of these books."

Liam just shrugged; he obviously was not ready to take on a bookworm in a bookstore.

We'd almost forgotten about the mother with the baby, but she'd not forgotten about us. In a flash she was in front of Liam and she pushed her baby up toward him and said in what might be her only words in English, "Money for the baby."

Not *food* for the baby, but "*money* for the baby," I thought. I suspected some kind of scam but it was likely that she did also need money and we were so disproportionately rich. I was confused and conflicted.

Then, it was as though in this extremely busy street everything paused or went into extreme slow motion and the light had an otherworldly quality. Even the dust was held in beams of sunlight. In my experience this happens an instant before a miracle is about to take place. Liam leaned down and simply kissed the baby. The woman's face lit up with a smile; she looked up at him and beamed.

He said, "You have a beautiful baby."

She said, "Namaste."

The woman turned away, everything sped up, and the woman was swallowed up in the busy street.

"What does 'namaste' actually mean?" asked Liam.

We'd already heard it a hundred times, but the woman said it with such fervency that we both really wanted to know what it meant.

I turned back toward the bookstore where the owner was standing at the threshold.

"I'm Ray and this is my friend Liam."

"Very pleased to meet you both. I'm Surendra." He put both his hands together over his chest.

"Surendra, can you tell us what 'namaste' actually means? We know it's a greeting, but not its meaning."

"Surely I can do that. Namaste means, I bow to the divine within you."

"Namaste," I replied, and Liam and I began to walk away.

I heard Surendra's voice from behind. "Perhaps you are interested in hidden places."

I wheeled around. "Yes, I am!" I replied instantly.

"Are you interested in them, Mr. Liam?"

"Not especially so," Liam replied.

I could have kicked him.

Liam continued. "I'm into wild rivers and big whitewater."

"You will both get what you are seeking," replied Surendra. I caught a big smile broadening across his face as he turned into his bookstore.

Then I distinctly heard, "You will both get even more than you are seeking." The laughter was swallowed up by the books and the noisy street.

Our next stop was the Shambhala Trekking Agency on the outskirts of town and close to the gigantic Boudhanath stupa. We arrived at the address on the Ring Road and there was no trekking agency; instead, there was the old Gopi Krishna Cinema Hall. I asked at the ticket booth and there was a long pause and a sigh. Finally the ticket agent said, "Yes, you are at the correct place. Go straight down the right aisle of the theatre and you will see the door."

The Mysterious Shambhala Trekking Agency

Liam led the way as we walked into the theatre. There was a Hindu movie playing at twice the regular volume, and a smattering of moviegoers. To the right of the stage was a small sign saying "Shambhala Trekking Agency." Inside was a very neat little office suite. There were three women in various small rooms. I said hello and introduced myself and Liam. The woman introduced herself as Anu. I then handed her the letter from Marie-Madeleine on Alexandra David-Neel's letterhead. She read it carefully and then turned it over a few times. She went and showed it to her colleagues. Using an intercom, Anu called in a few other people. I recognized the ticket agent and also the person that I walked by in the theatre. Now there were eight of us in the small suite; they were speaking together quite rapidly in Nepali and seemingly ignoring us. Liam and I looked at each other and smiled.

Anu turned to me and asked how I had met Marie-Madeleine, along with a lot of details about her appearance. I told Anu about my flight to Nepal and how I had been specially left a copy of *Magic and Mysticism in Tibet* by my father, who had been an explorer. She asked if there was any significance to my being named "Ray." I told her the short answer was yes. The questions went on for about forty-five minutes, and I could see that Liam, who was usually very patient, was growing restless.

"When are the questions going to end?" I asked.

"I just have one more question," Anu replied. "What is the nature of your Quest?"

I told Anu about Grandsy and how she was losing her will for life and how I believed that the answer would be found in the secret teachings of Shambhala. Anu and the others shook their heads in a sympathetic way.

Anu took a moment and looked around at the other women, and one by one they nodded their heads. Then Anu turned to me and said, "Ray, we're in agreement to help you on your Quest. Each of us has been trained at the Yalbang monastery to keep the location of Shambhala a secret and to ensure that others do not find the entrance. We have done this for thousands of years and you will find that we are very skillful at this. However, over the years we have allowed a small number of people to find Shambhala, to both fulfill their quests and to keep the legend alive."

"Why would you want to keep the legend alive? Surely it would be easier to keep it a secret if people stopped talking about it."

"Shambhala also exists in the imagination, and it is in these hidden places where magic is kept alive. So they must both exist and remain hidden to keep their power.

"We will send word to our ally Devi who is in Pokhara. You will meet her a week from today. Devi will spend many days with you to ensure that you are sincere in your Quest and that you will not reveal the location of the entrance under any circumstances."

I was handed another piece of paper, this time on Shambhala Trekking Agency letterhead. There was a flurry of bowing, laughter, and namastes all around.

Outside, Liam said we'd better head directly back and skip Boudhanath. I had wanted to see the world's largest stupa but mainly I'd been hoping to visit the Monkey Temple, which was called Swayambhunath.

Mum was pacing the courtyard and wanted to know why we'd been away nearly four hours.

I wanted to try to keep things positive and up front, so I replied, "Liam and I have made an amazing connection with a trekking agency that can guide me to the entrance of Shambhala."

Mum looked totally floored. So I added, "I mean, *us* to Shambhala."

This did not seem to help.

"You going to Shambhala. Why have I not heard of this before?"

"Well it started to come together in First Class--"

"May I remind you that you're accompanying us on a whitewater kayaking expedition and now you're talking about a trip to Shambhala. This is sounding more and more like your father. Let me remind you that you are sixteen, travelling with your mother, not organizing an entirely separate expedition. What's the name of this trekking agency that purports to be guiding you to Shambhala?"

"The Shambhala Trekking Agency."

"What? This sounds like one of your dad's fool's errand to yet another place that doesn't exist. Your Fa was a modern-day Don Quixote, and now you're following in his footsteps."

Don Quixote was a bit like Fa, I had to admit, but it was also one of my favourite stories.

"What's wrong with a hopeless romantic?" I asked.

"You'll find out."

But at this point, the fire had gone out of Mum. She was rarely negative about Fa around me, and I could see that it pained her to be so. I knew she still loved him but was protecting herself and me from further disappointments.

"Well, if this is the kind of Quest that Fa would have gone on, to just the place he so often spoke about, then maybe this is one of the best ways to look for him?"

"Oh, no, Ray, you're not pulling the Fa card on me again."

"Mum, no one else is looking for him."

Liam jumped in. "Our expedition team is meeting in Pokhara, and the section of rapids we hope to descend is on the Karnali--not too far from Yablang, the monastery where the nuns are based."

"What nuns?" Mum asked.

"The Trekking Agency is staffed by nuns from a particular monastery," Liam added.

"Really?"

I could see Mum was surprised. I let that sink in and then I added, "So it really won't be out of our way. First Pokhara and then the Karnali. Your trip fits right into my plans."

I gave them a broad smile so they knew I'd phrased it that way on purpose.

Mum turned her head and looked out at me sideways with a frown. It was a sign that she was watching me.

And there it was, barely imperceptible, a wink. I'm pretty sure Liam winked. I had another ally on my Quest.

Since we had only a month in Nepal, we were keen to leave Kathmandu as soon as possible. Especially since lung and viral infections were rampant; the city has no sewer system and few environmental regulations. But before we left for Pokhara, I was determined to see the Monkey Temple--Swayambhunath.

Meeting My Namesake

We decided to visit the Monkey Temple at dawn and then travel to Pokhara later in the day. We rose at five a.m., packed our bags, and left them at the front desk. We then travelled by rickshaw to just outside the Monkey Temple. We joined hundreds of Vajrayana (Buddhist) and Hindu pilgrims who gathered at the base of the dome, which represents all the earth. As the sun rose, it began to light up the stairway leading to the dome.

There was chanting and incense that contributed to the exotic and reverential procession. As I looked up, I got glimpses of two of the four sets of large eyes that look across Kathmandu in all directions. The eyes represent wisdom and compassion. Then glinting above the eyes, there is another smaller eye--a third eye--that is said to emanate cosmic rays that send messages to others to help them reach enlightenment. AND true enough, when the sun reached the eye near the top of the stupa, a ray emanated from it and lit the area on the staircase where we were standing. At that moment, all the pilgrims stopped. Mum, Liam, and I were in the light.

Okay, you can make light of it and say something like it was a "beam me up, Scotty" moment, but when you're named Ray? Likely after the ray emanating from the third eye and you are struck by a ray of light at dawn in Kathmandu with other pilgrims and believers, it's gotta mean something, or you're half-dead.

Above the beam coming from the third eye I could see thirteen golden rings spiraling upwards toward the top of the stupa, somehow I understood that these represented the realizations we go through to reach enlightenment. That Swayambhunath was one big temple to consciousness and mindfulness. But more than that it was a map . . . and maybe contained clues to entering Shambhala.

Just then, I felt a tug on my shoulder bag that jerked me backwards. I looked down and there was a monkey clutching my shoulder bag to its chest. But at this point I was too far off balance and was falling backwards. People quickly moved out of the way so I would not knock them over, but someone stepped forward and caught me. In the next moment I was looking into the most beautiful amber, almond-shaped eyes that I'd ever seen. I had the sensation that they were the same eyes that I was looking at on the temple. The young man held me for what seemed a long time and we gazed into each other's eyes. We were communicating through our third eyes. No language barrier.

"Who are you?" I asked.

"My name is Rai. I am a Honey Hunter, one of the traditional occupations of the Gurung tribe."

"My name is Ray, too, spelled Ray."

"My name is spelled Rai. It is traditionally a girl's name, but it is also another name for Vishnu--who is the God of Preservation and Protection."

"Is it a coincidence that we are meeting?"

"No. I'm here to warn you that there is danger in Shambhala."

"How do you know I'm interested in Shambhala?"

"Let's just say that I like Hindu movies."

"What danger could there be in paradise?"

"Paradises especially have their dangers."

"What's the danger?"

"I can't tell you beforehand."

"Why?"

"Because the gift is in its danger. I can't say more now. But I will keep an eye on you." He took a small dot that I learned is a *bindi* and put it on my forehead over my third eye.

A few moments later, I was upright, and Liam was coming down the stairs with my shoulder bag, and Mum was saying, "Ray, are you okay?"

Reluctantly, I broke the spell and replied, "I'm fine, I'm fine." I turned around to look for Rai. Then I heard his voice say directly into my mind, "See you again, Ray."

I was going to see him again. I'd met my own namesake. I was smiling inside.

The crowd started to surge forward, and we continued up the stairway. I should say I floated up to the top of the 365 steps. Once we arrived at the top platform, there was a gigantic *vajra*--a double-sided thunderbolt. We did a circumambulation around the top of the stupa a few times and saw a 360-degree view of the Kathmandu valley. There was too much smog to see the Himalayas beyond, but you could just imagine them rising up in the distance. Mum, Liam, and I took turns spinning the large prayer drums, and, without further incident, we returned down the steps. At the base of the stupa, the street was lined with rickshaws and a few taxis. We negotiated with an auto-rickshaw driver to take us to the bus terminal.

I've been to a few; my first wild bus station was in Nambia, and once you visit one, they all seem related. You must relax into the chaos and see the patterns. The patterns are not what you'd expect. Do not rush or you will not get on the right bus! That is the mantra.

Our TATA Beast

First of all, count yourself lucky if there is pavement. Sometimes it's just a big dirt area with no drainage and no pavement anywhere in sight. If so, you can be sure it rained overnight, the result being a gigantic wallow. The particular brand of beasts in Kathmandu are TATA beasts, an inexpensive bus manufactured in India. They have a reputation of spontaneously combusting. Kathmandu has recently started to retire buses more than twenty years old, so they are hardly what we'd recognize as buses in the Western world. They are more like indigenous animals; revving up, rocking back and forth, spewing black smoke, fishtailing, and sending up plumes of oil-laden mud onto anyone who manages to avoid being run down.

Second rule is, there is no obvious order as to how the buses are lined up and either no sign or an entirely misleading one as to where they are headed. There is no electronic or other board showing bus arrivals and departures, there is no obvious way to pay and get a ticket. This is a given, and it's best to adjust your expectations immediately.

Liam was utterly disoriented, and Mum was a bit overwhelmed.

Third rule, look for tea; do not aim directly for your destination, this is entirely amateurish. Sometimes the whole point of Third World transit is to expose the preoccupation Westerners have with a goal and a destination, even though it does seem obvious that the point of a transit system is to get somewhere. This is not so. The point of the system appears to be to teach Westerners that the journey is more important than the destination. If you manage to steer toward this tenet, you will survive; otherwise you will come out the other end a mess.

We needed a moment of calm; a port in a storm to figure out what's happening at this epic bus station. Oh, and it is epic because most of this country is not meant to have buses or motorized vehicles of any kind. Or anything with a wheel . . . the wheel was designed for automating prayers, not travel. However, the clever Swiss built many of these roads, and most of them just run up and down and zigzag over the faces of cliffs for ten to twenty hours. Oh, and the Himalayas are five times the height of the alps, Oh, and they were supposed to be paired with state-of-the art buses. Oh, Oh, Oh, then it makes sense that nearly every day you hear on the news there's been a bus disaster somewhere in Nepal. It's like hearing about the overnight killings in a big city: You come to expect it on the morning news.

It's something the Nepalese have come to expect. Nepalese roulette.

The chai wallah is that port in a storm. It's still before nine a.m., and there's that damp chill in the air. Steam is rising from a big metal caldron and the chai wallah hands you a battered tin mug that has probably been used by 10,000 people and then ladles you a steaming, creamy, spicy, Chai tea. You forget everything else as your hands cradle this hot nectar, then you put your nose to the lip and breathe in deeply. Euphoria.

The stress melts. Mum, Liam, and I look at each other and smile. In the midst of this seeming chaos, we have snatched a moment, and it gives us new eyes to see what's happening.

The buses are little islands strewn across a sea of mud. The buses are revving up and snorting and rocking back and forward and then gunning it and shooting forward to avoid getting stuck in the bottomless mud. Woe be it for anyone to get in the way of one of the departures. But what you also see if you look closely are passengers being ferried out to the buses by streetwise kids. So while still at the chai wallah, it was no surprise when a girl my age but smaller put her hand in mine and said the word "Ticket." I told her we had none. She pointed to a big crowd that was fanned out around what looked like a hot-dog vendor. We gulped down the chai, returned the precious mugs. She then led us to what we now realized was the ticket agent. After a few minutes, the hot-dog vendor / ticket agent called out to us across the crowd, "Destination, please!"

Liam bellowed out, "Pokhara!" There was a sea of nodding heads. Next the girl coached us to send a 100-rupee note out into the sea of hands that passed our money to the ticket agent. In return, our change and three battered old tickets that had survived many journeys and perhaps at this point were talismans of good luck were passed back across that sea of hands. It seemed like a miracle; perhaps not on the scale of Moses parting the Red Sea, but a miracle nonetheless.

Then, still holding my hand, she led us into the maelstrom of the pit. She was nimble, she was quick . . . we wove, we dodged . . . she kept to the high points of the pit, and we in our coloured clothing wound through this reddish-brown world. At one point, we travelled through a bus and out the back door. Finally, it seemed we'd arrived at the bus going to Pokhara. There was a boy on top of the bus whom we threw our bags to. On the bus, there was absolutely no room; even all the smaller-than-human spaces had live animals packed into them. The girl started to appeal to and then bully passengers so we could sit on makeshift seats up near the driver--supposedly coveted spots where you could see death approaching. We were then packed in like sardines. Mum handed the girl a twenty-rupee note, and the girl indicated she would wait atop the bus so that our luggage would be safe.

Not long after a door closed, the old TATA belched black smoke and started rocking back and forth. Moments later, we were charging through the pit, swinging this way to avoid both getting stuck and colliding with other buses. Through the smudged clearing in the window I could see people jumping out of our way. I must admit it was a tiny bit entertaining to see a tourist diving--well, slipping--into the mud to avoid getting run down. Finally, we ascended out onto the dusty road that would take us one step closer to our various destinations.

Besides the usual complaints of zero personal space and negative legroom, we were given roadside breaks while our on-board mechanic was repairing the bus. Fortunately, the bus broke down again just outside of Bandipur, and we were ferried into town by an army of rickshaws. The colourfully restored eighteenth-century buildings were delightful examples of local culture, and the main street was closed off and lined with cafés, lodges, temples, and an open market. We had been there just long enough to have lunch when we were told the bus was waiting for us on the outskirts of town.

Seven hours for a trip that was scheduled to be five hours was pretty good. Pokhara is a jewel to behold. Pokhara means "lake" and indeed it's a city of lakes and water. In the surrounding valley, there are eight lakes. It is also only a few hours from the very popular Annapurna Circuit and range of mountains. Up until 1960, there was no road from Kathmandu to Pokhara, and it was considered an even more mystical destination than Kathmandu. Mum immediately fell in love with the city. She wanted to visit the newly built World Peace Pagoda, and Liam wanted to try the new water-touching bungee-jumping site. I wanted to connect with Devi from the Shambhala Trekking Agency as soon as possible.

Initiation at Devi's Falls

There were over 300 lodges and hotels in Pokhara, a dizzying number of choices. I chose the Butterfly Lodge, of course, and after Mum looked through the *Lonely Planet* review, she agreed. It was only a two-star but it was clean, spacious, had a wonderful view of the Annapurna range, a communal garden, a good little cheap restaurant, and some of the profits went to a children's foundation. Oh, yes, and it was inexpensive. We threw our stuff down then threw ourselves on the beds. That's when Mum and I realized why it was not a three-star. Boing, boing.

I texted Devi and we arranged to meet the next day rather than in a week. Now here was my daring gamble that kind of emerged in the moment. Mum wanted to see the Peace Pagoda, and of course Liam wanted to go bungee-jumping. Separately, I told each of them that I was going with the other. Fortunately, a minor scene distracted them at breakfast, so no more details were discussed except our rendezvous time back at the lodge. That meant I was free to meet Devi alone.

It seemed quite natural with how things were named around here that we should be meeting at Devi's Falls, just on the outskirts of Pokhara. It's one of the main tourist attractions, and once I arrived there, I knew why. The fifty-metre falls is created by a high-volume river that flows from Lake Phewa over a series of cascades into a huge underground cavern and then disappears underneath Pokhara only to reemerge one kilometre away. The falls has a number of names, depending on who disappeared into its depths.

Just as I was looking down, marvelling at the cavern beneath the waterfall, a girl not much older than me with striking blonde hair just started talking to me.

"I know a way down to that cavern."

"Really?" I surprised myself by saying.

"Really," the blonde girl replied. "I'm Devi."

"Really?" I said yet again.

"Yes, really."

"But . . ." my voice trailed off. It was one of those embarrassing first conversations that do not start well.

"If we go off the trail over here, there's an entrance between those two boulders. I'll show you."

I was relieved Devi didn't question me further on my surprise at seeing someone who very much looked like a Westerner with the name "Devi" and yet part of a local trekking agency. I followed her as we left the official trail.

"How did you recognize me?"

"The agency texted me a photo."

The stairs were cut into the stone a very long time ago, and the opening smelled musty. I had to pay close attention to each step as my eyes adjusted to the light. As we descended, the passage grew cooler and wider until we came into a large cavern with stalactites. The smooth shapes of sedimentary rock created the most curvaceous and erotic stone patterns I had ever seen, and the water was like light flowing from above into a dragon's eye green pool.

"Do you want to know how people die at these falls?" asked Devi.

"No, but you're going to tell me anyway."

"They get lured into this water, and at the same time a floodgate on the dam above the falls is opened, and there's a surge of water."

I could understand the lure of these emerald pools. Before I knew it, Devi had undressed and quick as a flash she was in one of the pools.

I let out a gasp.

"Come on in!" Devi called out.

"No way!" I replied.

"I've checked--they do not plan to open the dam gates for the rest of the month. And here's a further incentive: Underneath Pokhara, the ground is literally porous. It's a maze of underground caves, caverns, and waterfalls, and one of the best ways to explore them is by floating along this underground river."

"What about our clothes?" I just had to ask the obvious.

"Of course I've thought of that. We'll just go a little ways downstream to give you a taste of the adventure that's right underneath everyone's feet."

I stripped down to my underwear and went in. I could see that Devi was impressed that I did not shiver or react to the cool water, which is something that Fa taught me to do.

The water was silky soft, like it was filled with minerals, and the sides of the pools and channels were worn perfectly smooth. I began to hear voices echoing from the cavern ahead. I grew alarmed.

"Are those voices?"

"Yes," replied Devi, "they are. Stay calm and we will just float through the pools. If people point at you, just smile and ignore them. If you don't, some tourist or devotee of Shiva will rescue you from the water and things will get messy."

"You knew this would happen!"

"Yes of course. It's an initiation. To gain entrance to the hidden realms, which are nearly always underground you must prove yourself and be able to listen."

"This is the initiation?" My voice was a little strained as I said this.

"This is one of the initiations."

"How many are there!"

"I can't say."

I took a guess. "There are thirteen, aren't there."

"How did you know that?"

It was great to hear a little bit of surprise in Devi's voice. "I know some things, too."

We were now floating along this subterranean river into a much larger cavern.

In the low flickering torchlight I began to see various gods carved into the stone walls of the cavern and maybe one hundred people, either pilgrims in prayer or tourists checking things out or clutching the metal railings, ascending or descending the stone steps.

"What is this place?" I asked.

"We're now in the Temple Cave of Gupteshwar Mahadev, or Shiva's Cave. Parvati is the wife of Shiva, and Devi is one of his consorts--time to wave."

We began waving and Devi was calling out, "I'm DEVI!" It took on this eerie resonance and echoed throughout the cave. There were gasps and everyone was motionless and straining to see us as we floated by. I decided to outdo Devi and called out, "I'm PARVATI!" We heard louder gasps just before floating out of the large chamber into a narrower passage where the water picked up speed.

"I have to say that was both fun, scary, and embarrassing. What was the purpose of that initiation?"

"One of the gatekeepers of this journey is being too self-conscious; but I prefer the word self-preoccupied, as self-awareness and consciousness are the only safe ways to gain entry to these hidden realms."

"How do you know if you are self-preoccupied? Aren't we all self-preoccupied?"

"No, some are very focused on others; there's a continuum. Yet for each journey there's a threshold. Had you been too embarrassed to go through what you just did, you would not have been ready. The gatekeepers ensure you are ready, that's it. You've just met and passed your first gatekeeper. But don't get smug. There will be others."

"Did you have to pass gatekeepers, Devi?"

"Many, many times."

We were gently floating through such a diversity of caverns along this subterranean river.

"Tell me, why are there so many caverns?"

"Because in a number of places on this planet, the earth is porous. Pokhara is one of these special places."

"What's the significance?"

"Wherever the geology is porous, subterranean secret societies have inhabited them and they become repositories of hidden knowledge."

"Last summer I encountered a subterranean city underneath the Kalahari Desert that was literally buried by the sands of time. It had become a giant hive where the Queen of the Queen Bees resides."

"Really, a giant hive, Honey . . ." and then Devi's voice dropped off. She was clearly being less forthright than usual. So I decided to keep my meeting with Rai the Honey Hunter a secret, at least for the moment.

I could see as we floated past many caverns and imagined the caves that led off them to be a honeycomb of secret meeting places and shrines.

"Only since 1970 have Westerners begun exploring this labyrinth of caves under the city. Still, it's largely unexplored, and many caves you must dive to get into."

"It's like there's a city under the hustle and bustle of the city, an inner city, a secret city," I replied.

"Yes, it's just like us humans--we have inner worlds that often go unexplored," replied Devi.

"Yes, I look around at many of my friends in Mt. Albert and they have a kind of claustrophobia."

"What do you mean?" said Devi. "I see the opposite--so many people are hunched in little boxes on their Xboxes. They have agoraphobia--fear of wide-open spaces."

"Oh, yes, I wholeheartedly agree. I mean a kind of fear of *their* inner spaces. Claustrophobia on the inside. They always have to be doing or watching something so they don't go inside themselves and view what's happening in their minds or their hearts."

"Yes," replied Devi, "so they get caught in those middle realms, between the inside spaces of their own consciousness and the big open spaces of the world around them."

"We see similar things." Our eyes met in a gentle embrace, our heads nodded, a smile echoed between us and I felt seen. What's more, were we were luxuriating in mineral-rich water, literally floating through hidden realms of space and seemingly through time . . . ancient time.

Before I was able to fully appreciate this, we started to tumble along an alarmingly steepening channel. I started to cry out and Devi shouted over the roar.

"Relax, Ray, relax!"

I saw blue sky at the end of the tunnel and now we were being swept along with no chance of grabbing hold of anything.

I yelled in a long, drawn-out expletive, "Are you *crazy?*"

Devi yelled, "*Geronimo!*"

At that moment, we shot out of the end of the tunnel and were part of the sky. Talk about lower-world upper-world experiences! It was instantaneous. My eyes had no time to adjust, and time stood still for a moment. Enough time to take in the beauty of the entire Pokhara lower valley; a string of jewel-like lakes, meadows, temples, laneways, and small, neatly laid-out fields. But it was looking down that really took my breath away. We were at least eight storeys up. I immediately went into a crouching position and began spinning.

Through the now whistling air and plummeting water, I heard, "RAY, RAY! Listen to me! You must form an arrow from toe to fingers and you must hold that form loosely. RELAX and all will be *well.*"

It was so difficult to open up--but as I did, I stopped spinning and my body righted itself as the air rushed by. Then, little by little, I relaxed all my muscles. I saw myself from outside my body entering the water below and hardly making a ripple.

Then my trance was broken by, "RAY, this is very important. Once you enter the water, you must open your body up like a parachute to slow yourself down."

I visualized myself doing this; I had no time to let fear enter. I knew that I must be all in. I took one last look around at all the beauty and took a deep breath.

I entered the water like a knife then immediately mushroomed open, that's when I nearly blacked out. My back hit what appeared to be sand, the water was filled with bubbles and I couldn't tell which way was up. Momentarily I was confused; then I watched the bubbles rise and followed them up. I burst to the surface gasping for air. I saw Devi swimming hard for the edge of the pool and I followed her. When I got to the edge, she pulled me right out in one amazingly strong, sweeping movement.

I didn't know whether to yell at her, hug her, or get the hell away from her. Just then Devi raised her arms to the sky, leaned back and yelled W-H-O-O-P-W-H-O-O-P-E-E! So I yelled, too--and we yelled it together--over and over, till the adrenalin transformed into endorphins, and we fell laughing to the sand.

"Don't ever do that again," I yelled in mock anger.

"You mean, *don't* ever *stop* doing that." She winked at me.

I just shook my head. I'd clearly got more than I'd bargained for.

Just then I realized that we were nearly naked. I just about panicked but managed to control myself and say in a fairly even tone of voice, "I thought you said we'd be able to get back to our clothes."

"I didn't say we'd get back to our clothes, I simply said, 'I'd thought of that.'"

"What does that mean?" Annoyance rising in my voice.

"It means that I've got clothes stashed over there."

From a hidden spot in the cliffside, Devi pulled out two beautiful saris.

"Now we can look like the goddesses we both are," Devi stated.

First we donned the slip and matching top that covers the shoulders, then Devi showed me how to wrap the sari; and then, as she put a bindi dot on my forehead, she said, "I give you your Nepalese name, Rashmi."

"I like it. What does it mean?"

"It means, 'Ray of Sunlight,' in Hindi."

It was a bit of a hike out from the falls, but we managed to find an auto rickshaw that was returning to Pokhara. I headed straight back to the Butterfly Lodge to see what trouble I'd stirred up, and Devi was going back to pick up our clothes. We'd meet tomorrow for the next "initiatory adventures," as Devi called them.

I'd hoped to return to the lodge before Mum and Liam returned from their adventures. However, when I entered the room, there was a note: "Come down to the garden right away."

Oh, Oh. I knew my mum's handwriting when she was upset. I decided to stay upbeat and pretend it was no big deal.

I saw Mum and Liam sitting in the Butterfly garden reading.

"Can I get you both a pina colada?" I asked.

"Sure," replied Liam

Mum shot him a look.

"Maybe later," he said smiling at me.

"Ray and Liam, this is serious."

"Don't include me in this," replied Liam

"Why did you lie to us both, Ray?"

"Well, I didn't really lie to you both because at the time I was not sure who I'd spend the day with. Then the person I was to meet from the trekking agency called, and that's when I decided to not go with either of you. So technically--"

"Technically! Do you think you're going to get off on a 'technicality'?"

"No, but I just thought I'd bring some perspective--"

"What about *our* perspective, when we returned and discovered that we both thought you were with the other person? Isn't that a legitimate perspective?"

Liam interjected, "Please keep me out of this."

"Why?" Mum replied. "Are you condoning Ray's behaviour?"

"No, but I feel quite differently about it."

"Really, how so?" There was an edge to Mum's voice.

I did not want Liam and Mum to argue over me. Or for Mum to even be able to hint that if they didn't work out it was because of an argument over me.

"Mum, I admit I should have been more straightforward and let you know where I was going."

"Yes, you should."

"But would you have let me go?"

"It depends."

"You see, it always depends."

"I let you come to Nepal."

"Yes but the restrictions were that I should be with you or Liam all the time. How can I have my own adventure and experience if I have to be following you both around? No offence, Liam."

"None taken."

"What do you think, Liam?" Mum asked.

"I'm not sure I should comment," Liam replied.

"We're all entitled to our opinion."

"Okay, I think that Ray should have more freedom to go on her Quest."

Mum shot in, "What Quest would that be? I'm getting pretty mixed up, here."

Liam looked over at me, hoping he hadn't spilled the beans.

"Of course," I replied, "the Quest to bring Grandsy back to life."

"Oh yes, *that* Quest. How did your meeting today connect with that quest?"

So I told them about meeting Devi at Devi's Falls and going into the cave, minus the river and the waterfall, of course.

"So is Devi leading you to Shambhala or to the secret of bringing Grandsy back to life?"

CHAPTER THREE
MUM GETS INTO BIG TROUBLE

Double Date at Ranighat Palace

Sometimes Mum seemed not to know how quests worked.

"Mum, they are related. Shambhala contains the key to longevity."

"Okay, so you say. But you are grounded in Pokhara for three days for lying to me. Liam is waiting for his team to arrive, and you're to stay at the hotel. I have my own announcement to make and have just now decided to say yes to an invitation."

"What is it?" I cried out. I glanced over at Liam, who was not so enthusiastic.

"Well, I have been invited to Ranighat Palace on a double date."

"Mum!" I looked over at Liam, who was trying to appear relaxed.

"You both do not think I'm adventurous enough. So I've decided to go on my own adventure, rather than just tagging along with you both on your adventures."

"Who is your royal date?" Liam asked.

"The two most powerful families in Nepal are the Shahs and the Ranas. Together, they own 50 per cent of the wealth in Nepal. The Ranas rule as the prime ministers of Nepal, and the Shahs are the royal family of Nepal, and in olden times they were seen as gods. Today at the Peace Garden I met Devyani Rana, daughter of the prime minister of Nepal."

"Is that who you are double dating with?" I asked with surprise.

"Yep."

"Who is your date?" Liam asked.

"Prince Paras."

"A real prince?" I asked.

"Yep."

I could see Mum was playing it cool and also toying with Liam.

"What's the catch, Mum?" I knew that she would not just agree to a date.

"Well, Devyani seemed such a fine young woman and she pleaded with me to join her. She said she and Prince Paras were secretly in love, but the Crown Prince, Prince Dipendra, who is next in line to the throne, was madly in love with her."

"It sounds like a Hindu movie," said Liam.

"In the Nepalese royal family, art obviously comes to life," I replied.

"It gets better than that. There's a century-old feud between the Rana and Shah dynasties. Each does not want the other to gain too much power, so the queen and king refuse to allow Prince Dipendra and Devyani to marry, which is fine with Devyani. So that's why she wants me to come on a double date with Prince Paras."

"So Devyani will be on a date with Crown Prince Dipendra and you will be on a date with his brother, who she secretly loves? Don't you see a problem with that?" I asked.

"Nothing that I can't handle," Mum said with a wink.

As the coming days would prove, nothing that my conservative Mum has ever said could have been so entirely wrong.

"While you're gallivanting around with princes, I should be at least able to wander around Pokhara."

"No, grounded right here. Everything you need is right here in this lodge. I don't want to be worrying about what you're up to when it's my turn to have a good time. That's final."

I looked over pleadingly at Liam, but he was not happy with this turn of events either, and just shrugged his shoulders.

I was pretty hungry, so I went over to the restaurant and ordered dal bhat followed by mango ice cream. Maybe I could survive here for a few days.

I was a little embarrassed to let Devi know I was grounded, so no "initiatory adventures" for a few days. But I told Devi that as Mum's away, she should come here and visit the Butterfly garden and we could eat at the restaurant and get to know each other better.

But Devi seemed to guess what had happened. "So the Butterfly Bard is grounded," she said laughingly. "Where's your Mum going?"

"Ranighat Palace."

"Very cool, that is one amazing place. A few years ago, I was kayaking along a remote stretch of the Kali Gandaki, and we came around a bend, and I saw built on top of a huge rock--a royal palace. There are caves in the rock and so many old arches on top of the rock that look like they go back hundreds of years . . . and then on top of that is a beautiful pale blue European castle. It looks like a fairy tale. We just had to camp on the beach below the rock and explore the palace.

"The story goes that in the late 1800s, the Rana general who built this palace staged a bloody coup by assassinating his uncle so his brother could become ruler of Nepal. It was successful, but once his brother became ruler, he banished his military brother. No relative would claim the palace because of the banishment. It was left to fall to ruin. Ironically it was locally called 'Rani Mahal,' literally meaning the 'Queen's Palace,' as it was built as a memorial of love for his wife. I've heard it's been partially rebuilt. But it's a full day's journey from Pokhara. How's your Mum going to get there and back in a weekend?"

"I think she mentioned a helicopter."

"Oh, oh. Helicopters in Nepal mean either the Rana rulers or the Shah monarchs or the military."

"Two out of three," I said quite proudly. Secretly, I was proud Mum had been invited to join Nepal's elite.

"Ray, this is quite serious. Most tourists don't know, and the country keeps it hidden, as the biggest source of revenue is tourist dollars, but Nepal is a powder keg. The Ranas and the Shahs have always been the fuse.

"Tell me exactly what your Mum is doing."

So I told her what Mum had told me. There was silence at the other end.

"Devi, are you there?"

"Yes, Ray. It could not be more serious than this. Your Mum has landed at the center of the powder keg and *she* just might be the fuse."

"I find that difficult to believe."

"Do me a favour: Trust me, based on the adventure we had together. Get your mum on the phone."

I wasn't sure I could trust Devi based on our adventure, but I left the restaurant and went back to the courtyard and asked Liam where Mum was. He said that a limo had picked her up an hour ago.

"Give me her number right away," said Devi, "and I'll call you back."

A few minutes later, I got a call back from Devi.

"Your mum is not answering; likely she is out of cell range. Here's some of the backstory that you and your mum are missing. Devyani Rana is really beautiful, intelligent, and modern, but she lives in a distinctly feudal society. Prince Dipendra is artistically inclined but is known to have a cruel streak and has been training with the paramilitary police and amassing the very latest weapons to make himself feel powerful. Likely he has the emotional intelligence of a five-year-old. Add to that, the king and queen of Nepal are desperately trying to hold onto power in a modernizing world and are thwarting his love for Devyani Rana. The Ranis are growing in power, as they have control of most of the military and also the political power. India is exerting its influence; Devyani's mother was born in India, and believe it or not, this is also a key factor in why they are against the marriage. Queen Aiswarya had already arranged a more suitable marriage for Crown Prince Dipendra--who is next in line for the throne. She is not going to let Devyani follow her as Queen of Nepal.

"AND, okay, now you are telling me that Devyani does not actually love Crown Prince Dipendra--she's in love with his brother, Prince Paras, and your mother is going on a double date to a Rana palace, which is founded on the assassination of family members to take over power in Nepal."

"So much for this sleepy little kingdom," I replied. "What can we do?"

"There's not much we can do at this point. But I will talk to my contacts and see if they have anyone in the area."

"Okay, swear to secrecy."

"I swear."

"What most outsiders do not know is that there has been a civil war raging in Nepal for fifteen years now; 19,000 combatants and civilians have died. The People's Liberation Front is fighting for a democratic Nepal and the abolition of the monarchy and the power elite and they are willing to do this by violent means. Currently, the PLF control over 60 per cent of the rural areas of Nepal. The Royal Army, led by the Ranas, refuses to fight the People's Liberation Front, so the civil war is between the police and the PLF."

"So what you're saying is there is yet another group destabilizing Nepal. Are these the Maoists I've heard about?"

"Yes."

"You're right, this is a powder keg, and Mum certainly has found her way right to the centre of it.

"And are you a Maoist? I just have to know, given the situation we're in."

"No, I'm called a Maoist sympathizer. I do believe in the intentions of the Maoists but I'm against using armed struggle to achieve it--more honestly, I'm a Buddhist, so I'm against taking life to achieve anything. As a known sympathizer, it's helped me to move through checkpoints and more freely around the countryside. It doesn't mean I'm safe. There are trigger-happy police, military, and also Maoists, and getting caught in an ambush or a firefight is always a possibility."

"Okay, thanks for sharing this with me. Given this tense situation, having someone I can trust is so helpful."

"Can you trust Liam?"

"Yes."

"Perhaps we should bring him in on this, then."

"Are you sure? What if nothing happens, and Mum just comes back on Sunday?"

"Trust me, that's pretty unlikely. Even though the Himalayas are dramatic, they are not half as dramatic as the Shah family. Best if we work on an exit strategy for your mum, then if she doesn't need it, that's great."

Devi came over to the Butterfly Lodge to meet Liam, and we went through the details of the political situation. The new information that Devi provided was that Mum's date was no lamb, either. Prince Para's drinking and late-night escapades in Chitwan were well known to Nepalis. He ran over a popular Nepalese singer, probably while intoxicated; as a member of the Royal family, he was not charged.

Devi finished by saying, "I know this must sound unbelievable to you, Liam and Ray; but don't forget that you in the West, especially in the US, have some pretty unbelievable political characters."

"I agree," said Liam, "but here we are now with Ray's mum in a potentially dangerous situation. What do you suggest, Devi?"

"We have no helicopter at our disposal, so I suggest we get as close to Ray's mum as possible--just in case we're needed."

"But I'm grounded!" I cried out.

"Well," said Liam, "I guess you better stay here and girl the fort."

"What!"

"Just kidding. We need you. I'm officially un-grounding you."

"You can do that?"

"Well, I just did it and I'll take responsibility for it with your mum."

"Whoopee, un-grounded!"

"What's the Plan?" I asked.

"Well," said Devi, "the Ranighat Palace will be heavily guarded, especially on this occasion, with both Ranas and Shahs present. And the palace was built by a military general and is nearly impregnable. And it's built on top of a rock."

"So, how?" I cried in exasperation.

"That rock is porous. Underneath the palace is the old palace, which is a catacomb of collapsing rooms and porticos. Perhaps there's a way in that way, I'm afraid I don't have all the answers yet; we'll have to make it up as we go."

"How long will it take to get there?" Liam asked.

"We can motorbike to Kailashnagar and then we'd need to walk for four hours. The trip would take a full day. But--and this is a big but--the Kali Gandiki runs right below the palace, and they would not be expecting anyone from the river, as there are some major Class V rapids upstream from the palace. And don't forget--the Kali Gandiki runs through the deepest gorge on earth."

"Did I not tell you Liam is a whitewater kayaker here on an expedition to run some undescended rapids on the Karnali called 'God's House'?"

"No, but I'd say that's a stroke of good luck."

"Are you in, Liam?"

"Hell, yes, I'm in! How do we get to the put-in on the Karnali?"

"There's a local flight--Pokhara to Belawa Airport."

"What about me? Can I run Class V rapids?"

There were simultaneous "Nos!"

"But," said Liam, "it's not entirely safe but I'll take Ray in a two-person kayak."

"Oh, YES, YES, YES!"

"I'll have to think about it, Ray. Your mum would not approve of me putting you in jeopardy without real just cause. Let's see if this escalates. We're just getting into position in case there is an emergency."

"That sounds right," said Devi. "Let's take it one step at a time. I will bring the Shambhala Trekking Agency into the loop and I'm sure, given the situation, they will arrange our flights and all transfers. Liam, you contact Charley Gaillard, who owns the only specialist kayaking shop in Nepal, Ganesh Kayak. He's a personal friend and will make sure you get everything you ask for. Just get everything to the Pokhara Airport for four p.m."

"That sounds great, Devi. I'll put together an equipment list and call him, as our own equipment does not arrive till Wednesday. My team is arriving over the next two or three days. Shall I ask them to wait here till we return or would it be helpful if they joined us?"

"Right now, I believe a small team is best. Fast and light--just how I like to climb."

"Wow," I replied, "looks like we got ourselves an adventure! Especially since a few hours ago, I was grounded. How sweet this is!"

Liam looked at me with a hint of concern.

I had really nothing to do but pack and research the Ranighat Palace. It's called the Taj Mahal of Nepal and it's built in European neoclassical style, one palace built right on top of the ruins of a much older palace, in a wild region where there are no roads.

All around me was a hive of activity; Liam and Devi made calls and came and went.

At two p.m. we had a meeting.

Devi began, "Our flight is arranged for five p.m. We will be in the air for only thirty minutes, and it will take us to the closest airport upstream from Ranighat Palace. However, it's still seventy kilometres from the palace; can we do it in a day?"

"Yes, but a very full day," responded Liam. "We'll need to overnight along the river tonight and then we can get an early start and be at the Palace before nightfall tomorrow."

"We would need to get there before dark."

"We can do that if we really push it. There are many Class III, IV, and a few Class V rapids along the descent that will really accelerate our travel speeds. Charley is great--he's a kayaker and he really knows what he's doing. We've arranged to get everything we need to the airport by four p.m. And I've got a good set of maps for each section of the river. I just need to pack my personal gear and I'm set."

"Great," said Devi. "I've made contact with the PLF (People's Liberation Front). I'm not sure they will be much help; they have not been based there for many years. The Ranas have renovated and staffed it.

"I'm packed and set. Let's make sure our watches and phones are synchronized. Okay, I'll be in an auto-rickshaw out front at exactly four p.m."

A National State of Emergency

Everything proceeded smoothly till just before we arrived at the Pokhara Airport. Horns were blaring, and people were shouting and crying in the streets. We stopped by a group gathered around a radio. There was an emergency report of a terrorist attack on the Royal Palace in Kathmandu. A few minutes later, when we arrived at the airport, the scene there was even pure pandemonium: No flights were leaving and all arriving flights were being rerouted to India. Devi phoned her father, Willi, who was the director of the Peace Corps in Nepal. Her father told her to get out of the airport as soon as possible. Briefly, she summarized my mother's situation and that she was presumed to be with two of the Royal Princes at Ranighat. Then Devi went silent; obviously her Dad was telling her what he knew. Then I overheard Devi repeat the word "massacre."

Devi was pretty white when she got off the phone a couple of minutes later. From Gurkha friends, Devi's dad had learned that all the members of the Royal family had been killed at the Royal Palace in Kathmandu.

"Thank God Mum's at Ranighat!" I all but shouted it out.

"We can't be certain of that," replied Devi.

"What do you mean?" Both Liam and I cried out at the same moment.

"We know that the Crown Prince and Prince Paras were in Kathmandu at the Royal Palace at the time of the massacre."

"How can that be? They were on a double date with Mum and Devyani Rana at Ranighat."

"Gurkha soldiers never lie--they are 100 per cent reliable. Dad's friend said they arrived by helicopter thirty minutes before the massacre."

"Oh, no! That means Mum might have been on the helicopter, too." I almost dropped to the ground. Liam caught me and held on.

"It means nothing of the kind," said Devi. "Dad's friend did not mention anyone else in the helicopter and he did say that although the entire royal family was dead, one of the brothers, Prince Paras, survived. According to eye witnesses, the Crown Prince killed his entire family and then attempted to take his own life."

"How could the Crown Prince kill his entire family? It sounds so unlikely," said Liam.

"I know, only in Nepal."

"How do you know it was not the Maoists or the Ranas?"

"Because the Gurkha officer told Dad that at the time of the shootings there were only family and relatives inside the palace. No one came or went."

"How come the Gurkhas did not stop the massacre?"

"You have to know the Gurkhas to understand. Their orders were to protect the Royal family from all outside threats but not to get involved in the affairs of the Royal family. The Gurkhas are known for obeying to the letter."

"So they did not intervene in a blood bath of those they were sworn to protect?"

"No," Devi replied. "However, their bravery and loyalty to following orders has won many battles for the British, who have entire regiments of Gurkhas."

"What's happening now?" I asked.

"The massacre appears to be over, Crown Prince Dipendra is in a coma and, ironically, is now automatically king, even though it appears he murdered his father, the king."

"So should we go to Kathmandu right away?" I asked confused by it all.

"No," said Liam confidently, "Either your Mum is now safe in Kathmandu or she may not have gone with them on the helicopter and she may still be in danger at Ranighat Palace. So we should go ahead as planned."

I looked over at Devi.

"That's a distinct possibility. The Ranas will be under great suspicion, and there may be retaliations. The Ranas came to power through a massacre (the Kot Massacre) and have ruled Nepal for over a century on the basis of brute force alone. I agree we should get to Ranighat with all haste.

"My Dad said we should immediately get out of the airport and onto the tarmac. There are four runways that are clearly marked. As you leave the terminal, look down and head for Runway One. He said he'd call in a favour he has with a Gurkha colonel and have him pick us up directly on the runway."

"What about our kayaks and gear?"

"Look," said Devi, "It's unusual to see a float plane in Nepal and there's one idling at the threshold of Runway One, so that must be for us. We have no time to find our gear in this chaos. We're just going to have to improvise."

"Swell," said Liam with a smirk. "I'm up for improvising."

Colonel Lachhiman and His Flying Machine

The three of us made a dash across the tarmac into the waiting float plane.

The pilot was waiting at the door, "You must be Devi, and these must be your friends. I'm Colonel Lachhiman. I see you have made a good call and not brought your equipment. Please step inside, sit down, and strap in for immediate takeoff."

Colonel Lachhiman moved quickly, closing the door of the Cessna and then strapping himself into the pilot's seat. Somehow, I ended up sitting in the co-pilot's chair. Lachhiman paused and looked over at me. Our eyes met, and I held his gaze.

"What's your name?" he asked.

"Ray."

"Right, I'm going to call you by my niece's name, Rashmi, which means Ray of Light. Is that okay with you?"

I looked over at Devi and smiled and then looked back at Lachhiman and nodded my head.

"That will do perfectly well."

"Rashmi, I'm going to teach you how to fly and to land this plane."

All I could say was, "What?"

"Perhaps you mean 'Why?' I can answer that. It is your mother that we are rescuing, is it not?"

"Yes, it is."

"Then you are most motivated to learn and you are responsible for these others coming on this mission--are you not?"

"Yes, I am. But why would I need to learn to fly this plane?"

"Because there's a distinct possibility that I may become incapacitated during this flight. However, we must leave this airport while it is under civil authority, and I will tell you more en route. Is this agreeable to each of you?"

We looked over at each other. Each of us felt the seriousness and urgency of Colonel Lachhiman's statements. We nodded our heads.

"I can see you're in agreement; so, Rashmi, watch what I do closely. There are dual controls. Do exactly what I do on the yoke and with each of the switches. I have completed the preflight checklist before you arrived.

"Tower: Request clearance for takeoff on Runway 1."

"Tower--request denied--we're under lockdown."

"Pokhara Tower, Cessna VC Cross, ready at Runway 1."

"Cessna VC Cross permission denied. Power down and exit the runway."

The Cessna engines were now running full throttle and it was lurching forward.

"Pokhara Tower: This is Colonel Lachhiman of the Gurhka Rifles. I do not recognize civilian authority; proceeding with takeoff."

Colonel Lachhiman turned to us as he released the brakes and pulled the throttle out to full. "Don't be concerned--the security at the airport will not fire on us without military authorization."

Just then, we saw the door of a hangar open and a fire truck came racing out toward the runway, obviously trying to block us.

"However, the fire department is a civilian department. They will be able to block the runway and prevent us from reaching the takeoff zone."

"Is that it, then?" I asked stunned.

"There is another runway under construction."

"Go for it!" we all shouted.

Lachhiman managed a sharp turn at high speed, and we were bouncing around on the bare dirt. The fire truck was veering toward us and gaining on us. We made it onto the runway threshold.

We all shouted, "But it's not finished!" There was a giant asphalt-roller on the runway right in the takeoff zone.

Lachhiman pulled the throttle out all the way, "That's what I was telling you."

The twin engines roared to life. The fire truck was hurtling toward us; fortunately, the runway was now in the opposite direction of the oncoming fire truck. It was clear that the fire truck was going to drive us off the runway or crash into us. Just moments before impact, the Cessna started to outpace the fire truck. Now all our eyes were focused on the asphalt-roller.

"Now, Ray, when I give the signal, I want you to pull back on the yoke with all your strength. I will pull this parking brake-like control that operates the flaps. If we do this together, the Cessna should be able to manage a short hop at this speed. Brace yourselves for a jolt."

Just before hitting the roller, Lachhiman gave the order, and I pulled back with all my might, the Cessna lurched unhappily into the air and then dropped down just on the other side of the roller. We bounced and skidded sideways before he got the Cessna under control again. We then roared down the runway for another couple of hundred feet before we both gently pulled back on the yoke and smoothly rose from the runway. I looked down at the fire truck and the roller that moments before loomed so large; they were now growing smaller by the second.

"Whoopee, that was close!" shouted Devi.

"I'm not sure that's a good thing," commented Liam.

"Sure it is!" said Devi. "Look how alive we're feeling right now. That feeling's a good thing. My dad and I have lived for that feeling since I was young."

I did feel very alive, but I guess I still had Mum's voice in my head saying there's only so many times you can feel this way without one of them being the last.

Devi could see that I was hesitant.

"Ray, I choose this feeling, and when it's my last time and there's no way out, I know that I'll be on my way to the next lifetime of adventure. I am choosing short lifetimes of adventure rather than what I see around me: living deaths ruled by fear and increasing caution."

Liam said, "I guess I'm trying to find a balance between risk and responsibility."

Colonel Lachhiman piped up, "I stay away from all those confusing questions, as I have devoted my life to duty: duty to my family, to other Gurkhas, and my allegiance to whoever's in charge. When I am under orders, I follow those without question. That's the Gurkha way."

"But--" I was about to jump in.

Lachhiman interrupted me. "This is no time for a moral argument. I will not change in this lifetime; this is the way of the Gurkha. Perhaps next lifetime I will be like you, a free moral agent. Right now we must discuss our plan. The massacre in the capital, and, Ray, your mum's precarious situation, demand we get to Ranighat Palace as soon as possible. I chose this float plane--the only military float plane in Nepal-- so we will have the opportunity to land on a widening of the river upstream of the palace.

Liam said, "I didn't know you could land on a river."

"In an emergency you can attempt to land anywhere its possible."

"Is it possible," I asked.

"Yes," replied Col. Lachhiman, "It's possible."

Liam had his maps out and had found the widening in the river just upstream of the palace. "But there are a set of big rapids between the widening and the Palace."

"Yes, I know but Devi's Father also said you, Liam are an expert kayaker and I'm guessing you'll be able to find a route through those rapids."

"For a Cessna!" Liam's voice was rising.

"Yes, and you must relay those instruction to Ray who will be using the rudders to steer the plane."

"Where will you be Col. Lachhiman?" I asked in surprise.

"I will be unconscious."

"Unconscious!" We all shouted in unison. This certainly was a series of surprises.

"Yes, I am under direct orders not to land this plane anywhere except at Tribhuvan International Airport. However, as Devi's Father is a friend of mine I cannot turn you in to the Nepalese Military. However, I do have a unique ability to hold my breath till I go unconscious. I have done this before on missions to appear dead. This way I will not be landing the plane or even consciously present. When I go unconscious you Ray must take over the controls and land the plane. My orders do not state that I cannot take off or fly so I will be waiting in the plane and can attempt the difficult take off when you return from your mission."

We were all a bit stunned by this, but one thing we were sure about was that Col. Lachhiman was serious and he could not be argued out of his position. If there was a better plan none of us could think of one.

"Are there any more surprises?" Asked Devi.

"Perhaps, maybe just one more. The widening will give us enough space to land but we must fly through the gorge for me to get Ray into position to land on the river. As you might know the Kali Gandiki is the deepest gorge on earth. We will have to fly under a suspension bridge and then drop close to the level of the river and follow the canyon for a few miles.

Despite the fact that there are no roads in this region, you can be sure that security has radar that they are monitoring. This way we'll be undetectable and have the advantage of arriving at Ranighat without warning."

Looking at me, Liam said, "Somehow my whitewater adventures seem tame after what you and your mum dish up."

We all had a good laugh at that.

Colonel Lachhiman went through the basics of flying a float plane: When you are in level flight, the engine cowling is level with the distant horizon; above or below this, you are ascending or descending; it is important to look at the artificial horizon gauge to see if the plane is level or banking; the plane basically flies itself if you don't touch the controls. I got a chance to reduce the throttle and engage the flaps--the parking brake-like lever--just to feel how the plane slows down.

Once I got used to the basic controls for flying the plane, Lachhiman went over the following procedure: "When the plane is about twenty feet above the landing area, cut the power to zero and gently lift the nose above the horizon. Now the plane will begin to settle. The controls get mushy at low speed, so be prepared to use more exaggerated adjustments to keep it straight. To prevent the floats from catching, raise the nose by pulling all the way back on the yoke just until the plane touches down. It's as simple as that, no problem with current at this point, as you'll be moving fast."

"Next comes the tricky part," added Liam.

"Yes, sir, right you are about that. I have not heard of anyone running rapids in a float plane. But you do have some control. Activate the water rudders on the floats (the catch is on the floor between the seats). You must do this as soon as possible. Do not use more than one-third throttle to manoeuvre, as you will take a nose dive with too much power. Then follow Liam's exact directions to take you through the rapids. Do not be surprised at how large they are. Just after the rapids, kill the ignition and float down toward the palace. It's on a tight bend, so you will come close to shore. I suggest Liam swim ashore with a rope.'

"Hey," said Devi, "I'm a pretty good swimmer, too, and I don't think Liam should get all the choice jobs. Let's play stone, rock, scissors for it."

"You're on," said Liam.

I looked at them; I could not have been more fortunate to be on an adventure with these two. Even though the stakes were high, they were still willing to be playful. No matter how tough things got, I knew I could count on these two. What a relief that was!

Devi beat Liam at paper, rock, scissors.

Colonel Lachhiman pointed out the bridge below us and said that we were within five miles of the palace.

"You," said Lachhiman, "are going to fly under that bridge. Of course, I'm right here on the other yoke, but I trust your judgment and abilities."

"I'm pretty sure flying under bridges is against the law everywhere," commented Liam.

"It's a good thing I didn't swear allegiance to civil law," Colonel Lachhiman reminded us with a twinkle.

I pulled back on the yoke and started to turn us toward the bridge. I kept adjusting the throttle to keep our wind speed constant, keeping my eye on the artificial horizon. I used the flaps to slow us down as we lined up for the bridge. It was growing larger, and I could see it right above the engine cowling. We were on a direct intercept course with the bridge. Then I gently dropped the nose below the bridge and got us lined up. All of us were checking for snags and overhanging wires. We held our breaths as the Cessna roared under the bridge and we were about to let out a cheer when we looked ahead and saw the canyon narrow and deepen. Our plane was like a speck in this vast landscape. The black cliffs towered and wept with waterfalls and below us the wild green dragon of a river slithered over boulders the size of houses.

Ray and the Magnificent Flying Machine

"Relax, Ray," stated Colonel Lachhiman. "Relax and enjoy the beauty and the fluid movement of this little plane. Do not think of what is next; just be in this moment, and you'll discover how precious this edge is. How you are most alive here. I can tell that Devi knows and treasures this edge, and now it is your turn to be conscious of this place and learn to be at home here. This is being alive; the rest is a kind of sleepwalking."

I was starting to feel what he was saying; it was a kind of fully awake trance. Like all of my brain woke up and whispered, "We are here." Who was "we"? Perhaps it was my relatives who had passed away? Or perhaps it was Grandsy? Somehow, all the way over here, she had my back.

"I'm getting the hang of this," I said to Col Lachhiman excitedly. When I got no response, I turned toward the pilot seat and there he was, quietly slumped over with a serene look on his face.

I glanced at Liam and Devi in the seats behind. Devi winked and Liam gave me the thumbs-up. It was up to me.

"Devi and Liam, can you unbuckle Colonel Lachhiman and buckle him into the rear seat? Liam, I want you up here to help navigate the rapids."

I tried not to remember that I was sixteen, had never flown a plane before, and now had to fly through a canyon and land on a narrow ribbon of water. If others trusted me to do this, then I can, I told myself.

There was a sharp turn to the canyon and I banked the plane hard to avoid the immense, thousand-foot wall of rock. One more turn and we began to see a widening in the canyon through the narrow walls. We flew toward the light. I brought the plane closer to the river and slowed us down, but just before the canyon opened up, we were hit by a blast of air that knocked us down. I pulled up on the yoke and pulled hard on the throttle. We barely missed crashing into the river and now were in danger of flipping. I wrestled to bring us flat to the artificial horizon but we were now ascending too steeply and in danger of stalling. I kept fighting what Liam reminded me was a katabatic wind.

Once we were through the narrowest part of the canyon, the winds abated, and I got us back down to river level. As the canyon widened into a flood plain, the river began to meander. Just before the end of the valley, I could see a relatively straight stretch and a widening.

I thought I said to myself, "I hope it's deep enough, I hope it's deep enough," then I realized I was talking to myself out loud.

I was totally focused on that spot. I lined up the top of the engine cowling, dropped our speed to just above stalling, made sure we were absolutely flat to the horizon, lowered the flaps, and, at the last second, pulled hard up on the yoke. We dropped like a duck onto a pond.

"YEAH!" Liam and Devi cheered.

I engaged the rudder and gave us some manoeuvrability with the throttle and started to navigate down the river to where the canyon narrowed again. As we got closer, we could see the river narrow and the rapids build. The standing waves were larger than the plane.

"You can do this," Devi whispered to us both.

"Snag, hard starboard," said Liam.

"Woya, pilot," I replied, "let's keep it in English."

"Okay, landlubber, hard right."

We were in them now. Like a child's toy dropped into a spring flood. The walls closed in and it grew darker. Every time we rose up to the crest, Liam leaned forward, eyes straining to see ahead.

Hole, hard left. Huge drop, stay left. Huge rock, hard right. Keep to the centre channel. Hazard, go left . . . and so on and so on. Suddenly, we were through the long stretch of rapids and the canyon had widened again. I cut the engine and after the roar of the plane and the rapids, there was silence. I looked back, and Colonel Lachhiman was still slumped over with that peaceful expression.

We gave each other a spontaneous high five as we floated down the river.

Devi shouted, "Look!" and pointed to the rock on the bend ahead. There on top of it was perched Ranighat Palace, aflame in the evening light. My first glimpse gave me the impression that it was a European palace built on top of an ancient monastery. It felt like this was the true home of my spirit. Looking at it, I had a sense of calm abiding, that nothing could go wrong in this place of monks and rulers. Then I vaguely remembered something in social science class about the importance of separation between church and state.

The palace was looming larger, and we were approaching the sharp bend. We could see no guards on the river side. Devi stripped to her underwear.

"Devi," I said, "how come on each adventure you end up in your underwear?"

"Haven't you heard of the goddess Inanna? Looks like I'm living out her story over and over."

I remembered something about Inanna having to remove a piece of clothing at each of the seven gates to the underworld.

"Liam," said Devi, "there's no need to look away. It's only my underwear. Hand me the rope from over there."

Devi took the rope, opened the door, manoeuvred out onto the pontoon, attached the rope to a cleat on the pontoon, grabbed one end, said, "Wish me luck," and plunged into the river. She swam hard and still made little progress against the current. Ten minutes later, just as we were passing the point, Devi dragged herself onto the shore and stumbled up to a tree and tied the rope to it. Immediately, the rope pulled taut and swung the plane around. As hard as Devi pulled she could not move the plane against the current. Liam stripped down and used the line to pull himself to shore. He then hauled with all his might, and still they couldn't move the plane to shore. I thought, *why do I need to strip down to my underwear in this adventure, too--and just before entering my palace? Next adventure, I want some more dignity!* But strip I did, and, thanks to Fa, jumping into the icy cold water was not so bad.

All three of us hauled on the rope attached to the float plane, easily moving it toward shore. Then I looked over at Devi and Liam, and they were quietly laughing.

"I suppose that invading the palace in our underwear is out of the question," giggled Devi.

"At least let's get a dry pair of underwear," I suggested.

I could see that Liam was not all that comfortable and he climbed into the cockpit and was scrambling and falling trying to get his clothes on without drying himself properly.

We got Liam to hand us our overnight bags from the plane. Then we asked him to retrieve this and that from the plane.

"How's Colonel Lachhiman?" I asked.

"Still out cold," Liam replied.

Above us was the beautiful outline of Ranighat Palace against the last light of the evening sky. The moon was already high, and it was like a mini-day within a night. For extra light, Devi and I had our headlamps on and our makeup laid out on the rocks. On the sandy beach, we had improvised a powder room. When Liam asked if it was okay for him to come out of the plane, not without a hint of annoyance, we told him that a woman's powder room was no place for a man like him. More giggles.

In a frustrated voice, Liam said, "What the hell's going on? We're here to rescue your mother and my friend, and you two are dressing up like it's a graduation party."

"Liam, Liam. Dear, dear," said Devi, in a humorously condescending way.

"Show us your weapons and your plan for breaking into a well-fortified, guarded palace. Why do men place such high value on 'storming the gates'? Your bravado will do little more than get us put into a prison cell."

"What's your plan?" asked Liam, brightening up. "I guess I've been worried about the likelihood of us succeeding in breaking into the palace, but I was not sure if there was any other option."

Devi and I looked over at each other. We hadn't formulated a plan, either. It was just that we both knew not to try to take the palace by force but to use more surreptitious means.

"We're simply going to walk in the front door. The unlikelihood of two well-dressed young woman just appearing where there are no roads and no helicopter landing will give us the element of surprise. That will give us enough time to read what's happening in the palace. If Devyani Rana is there, she will be our ally."

"What happens if it's the paramilitary?" asked Liam.

"Then I'll play the 'Dad'' card. My father, Willi, is the head of the Peace Corps in Nepal. It will give them pause, as the US protects the families of their nationals who are working abroad."

I put in, "My dad is a mystic adventurer who disappeared five years ago. I could play that card."

Devi and Liam did not laugh but came over and gave me a hug.

Devi and I finalized our outfits.

"What do I do while you two are taking the palace by powder storm?"

"You," said Devi, "have the most important role. Our passports must not fall into police or paramilitary hands. You must not get caught under any circumstances. If we do not come out of the palace in two hours, you must go with Colonel Lachhiman and tell journalists where we are being held."

"I'll keep your passports safe and I'll find a high point to keep an eye on you both."

Devyani: Jewel in a Crooked Crown

We carried our shoes and walked barefoot up the steep, winding path that took us from the beach up the rock face and around to the front of the palace. Liam gave us both emotional hugs. We put our shoes on and walked from the shadows, onto the grand path lined with flowering rhododendrons, right to the front door. No one was there, so Devi lifted the huge iron knocker, looked over at me, and said with a wink, "The game's afoot," and struck the door hard.

Moments later, it flew open, and there were two guards dressed in paramilitary outfits and with submachines levelled at us.

"That is no way to treat invited guests," said Devi in a remarkably calm voice. "Tell Devyani that her friends from America are here and are not very happy at having weapons pointed at them."

The weapons were dropped immediately and there were several, "Sorry, Madams."

The guards rushed off, and we were left standing there. In the distance, we could hear a celebration going on. A few moments later, the guards came down the stairs with Devyani Rana. She was elegantly attired but obviously had been crying. Devyani scrutinized us with her eyes and we returned her gaze. After a moment she turned to the guards and warned them not to disturb anyone at the party. These were her guests and she'd take care of them in the upstairs sitting room. They nodded their heads and went back to their posts at the main entrance.

Devyani grabbed my hand and said, "You must be Ray--I've heard all about you from your mother."

"Is my mother safe?" I let out with a gasp.

"Yes, she's safe; you'll see her in a minute."

I can't describe my relief. Fortunately, Devi was there to hold me up on the other side, or I would have just dropped to the floor and sobbed.

"We are not safe yet," Devi reminded me.

I straightened myself up and introduced Devi to Devyani.

Devi told Devyani, "I have it from a reliable source that Prince Paras has survived."

Now it was Devyani's turn to gasp and need our support. Tears were streaming down her face as she led us through the maze of rooms upstairs and then though large French doors into a room where Mum was waiting. We ran and threw our arms around each other. I felt something in that moment that has taken me years to understand and feel again that intensely. It was love, pure and unconditional. We each would have given our lives for the other. Absolutely nothing else came close to mattering. All the little squabbles were nothing compared to this. We pulled each other so close in the desire to melt right into each other's heart. Because in fact we were not separate.

After a few moments, Devyani said, "You both must be hungry."

Devi and I nodded. Devyani pulled a cord, and a few moments later, a servant appeared from behind a wall. Devyani ordered that some plates from the feast be brought upstairs with refreshments.

Mum and I sat next to each other on the big couch and held hands. There was also an instant bond between Devi and Devyani, who also held hands. We shared what we knew.

Devyani told us how her family could not believe its good fortune and were celebrating that their archrivals, the Shahs of Nepal, are now history. "It's so ugly; they are toasting me, saying that my love triangle has accomplished in a year what over hundreds of years of rivalry could not do--bring down the Shah Monarchy.

"And," Devyani sobbed, "it's true."

"It's not true," said my mother.

"No, it's absolutely not true," I said. "You are absolutely not responsible for Prince Dipendra's actions! That he fell in love with you and then resorted to violence is his own twisted behaviour. It just does not add up that because you did not love him, he massacred his family."

"And," said Devi, "that his family was so manipulative of who he was to marry and that they encouraged his acquisition of the latest assault weapons just shows how twisted the family was."

Mum added, "We women must stand together and love who we wish and not take the blame for the violence of men!"

We all held hands and sobbed above the escalating celebrations below. We all could sense that right underneath us the party was getting out of hand.

Devyani said, "My family also is heavily armed. I would not be surprised if a few bullets came through the floor to dislodge me from upstairs and encourage me to join the celebrations below. Also, the guards will have reported your presence to the chief of security and he will report to my uncle. By the way, how did you get here?"

"Yes," my mum asked, "how did you get here?"

"By plane," stated Devi.

Devyani looked at us incredulously, "Did you parachute here?"

"No, float plane," I replied. "We landed on the river."

"Wow, that's never been done before," said Devyani.

I could see that Mum also was very impressed.

"And, it was Ray who landed the plane," added Devi.

Devyani looked impressed, and Mum looked incredulous.

"Can we escape the same way?" asked Devyani.

"That's Plan A," said Devi.

"Well, I suggest," said Devyani, "that we take the servants' passage down to the old palace beneath us, then along an old secret passageway through the rock to the beach. It's risky, but I bet that's no big deal for you two adventurers. This way, the guards won't be alerted to our leaving."

Devi suggested to Devyani, "Before we leave the room, can you send an 'all-clear' signal to our friend Liam by flicking the sitting room lights? He'll be worried, and we're close to the two-hour mark."

I replied, "Make sure you don't do three long, three short, three long, or you'll be sending the SOS signal, and our Gurkha pilot, Colonel Lachhiman, will come storming in here and slay everyone with his knife."

"Ray," Mum replied, "this escapade has evidently brought out a darker sense of humour."

"Something like *M*A*S*H*," replied Devyani, "It's very popular over here."

Devyani signalled with the lights before we slipped behind the false wall into the servants' passageway. The staff were so busy that they basically ignored us as we wove our way down through the palace to the kitchen. We went through the busy kitchen, which smelled so wonderful that I wanted to stay there. Devyani signalled us to follow her through an old door that was clearly not part of the new palace. It took us down to the wine cellar, where there was an even older door. Try as we might, it would not budge. It was either locked from the other side or it was bricked up.

"It must have been closed up to stop the staff from escaping with the stores," said Devyani.

Just when we were giving up hope we heard some sounds from the other side and then the door swung open. It was Liam. I'm glad he came through for us at that moment, as I wanted him to be the hero in Mum's eyes. They hugged, and I could see their eyes shining.

Devyani was briefly introduced to Liam, and he led us out through the labyrinth of grand old rooms that were the old palace. I would have loved to explore this time warp of faded glory. Finally, we entered a narrow, rounded, stone passage that was dripping with water. Toward the exit, we could see moonlight and the beach--and there was Colonel Lachhiman leaning against the float plane, smoking a cigarette. This was the Nepalese version of *Casa Blanca*.

We were about to introduce Colonel Lachhiman to Devyani and Mum when Devyani in an urgent voice reminded us that someone on staff would have let security know about us leaving. Liam took off toward the tree that anchored the plane at a run. It was not a moment too soon, as security started pouring out of the passageway from the rock. We made a beeline to the plane. Fortunately, they were reluctant to fire, as they knew that Devyani was with us. But they showed no such reluctance toward Liam, who was now sprinting toward us. Col. Lachhiman and I were in the pilot and co-pilot seats.

"No pre-flight check," I said.

"Agreed," replied Lachhiman.

We were floating away from the beach, and you could hear the bam-bam-bam of assault rifles and the ping, ping as they ricocheted off the plane. Liam was running through the shallow water and then dove and swam with all his might toward the plane. Colonel Lachhiman was keeping the throttle just above idle so we moved away from the beach but still gave Liam the chance to swim toward us.

Colonel Lachhiman told me to head downstream.

"It's more risky, as we'll need more speed for takeoff but it will take us away from the weapon fire."

I was not about to argue. Just as I'd swung the float plane downstream, Devi and Devyani reached down and pulled Liam straight up onto the pontoon, and all three of them dove into the plane and slammed the door to the sound of the bullets pinging on the water and the plane. Lachhiman gave us nearly full throttle, and I lowered the opposite flap to counter the force of the twisting prop.

"Where did you learn that trick?" asked Lachhiman.

"Basic physics, I guess."

We were picking up speed fast, but our speed over ground was not increasing as quickly as the water was also accelerating. Ahead, the river narrowed and the cliffs soared as the Kali Gandiki headed into another deep gorge. We were starting to bounce across the wave tops, but the height and speed of the rapids was also increasing, and we were ploughing through Class V standing waves. As we increased in speed, the waves we ploughed into were becoming harder, and we were being thrown around. If we had not been strapped in, we would have been thrown out of our seats. The plane was being pounded, and it felt like it was being torn apart. Our eyes were glued to the front windscreen and the narrow canyon walls dead ahead. I had the elevator controls all the way back. Normally in this position the plane will lift off by itself when the floats start to plane, but this was anything but normal.

Airborne

Col. Lachhiman said, "We're going to have to use that big standing wave ahead as a ramp. To do that, we will have to use the ailerons to unstick us from the water, and simultaneously use the elevator controls to give us some back pressure to lift us up."

I adjusted the rudders to aim the plane at the biggest standing wave Liam had seen. The pontoons ploughed into the massive standing wave and, just as the propeller began to chew into the wave, they rose up, and our little Cessna hurtled upwards to the crest. But the wave was a real kicker, and we were now at too steep an altitude. At that height, Liam could see that there were giant trees stuck between the canyon walls blocking any possibility of our flying through the canyon. Just as it seemed there was no hope, and I could see everyone was white-knuckling it, Colonel Lachhiman banked the plane, nearly stroking the canyon walls with our pontoons, dipping the right wing in the river, creating the sharpest bank I could have ever imagined, literally pirouetting the plane and then flattening it out a few inches above the water, where we roared upstream past the castle and into a steep climb above the canyon. No bullets this time, as a hit to the engine would have killed the Rana passenger.

There were hugs and congratulations all around, as this rescue would not have been possible without all of us. And yet the joy was muted as we felt Devyani's loss and the senseless tragedy surrounding it.

As we headed away from the palace, I asked Lachhiman what he needed to do.

"Thank you, Rashmi, for asking."

"None of this would have been possible without your remarkable abilities and character."

"After I came to in the plane, I had a chance to give it some thought. Devyani's uncle is a general, one of my highest commanders. I have decided to devote my services to his niece for the time being, and anything she decides is my command."

We all cheered at his announcement. None of us wanted to return to Kathmandu under arrest or get into the complex logic of Colonel Lachhiman's ethical system.

First we asked Devyani what she wanted to do. She had relatives on her mother's side in India. She would be taken in there and she could decide what her next move would be from that safe haven.

"But where would *you* like to go?" Devyani asked.

I looked at Mum. "What do you need?"

"A little less adventure for a short while."

"I can understand that," said Liam

"But dear, having seen how you are under pressure, you are obviously an adventurer like Fa. I want you to fulfill your Quest. I trust you, and you have my unconditional blessing and support."

"Wow, I never thought you'd say that! Devi, what's our next stop on our way to Shambhala?"

After a few minutes, it was decided that Devi and I would use the parachutes and would bail close to Yalbang Monastery (that Mum agreed to this is a miracle). Then in only fifteen minutes' flying time, Colonel Lachhiman would land at Simikot Airport and drop Mum and Liam off where Liam had planned to rendezvous with his kayaking team. Then, fuel up the Cessna and fly Devyani to Haridwar--just over the border into India, where her mother's family lives.

Mum and Liam were meeting his whitewater team at Simikot and then they would hire porters to carry their gear to the put-in on the Karnali. Devi and I would rendezvous with them at "Upper God's House" on the Karnali, right between Yalbang Monastery and the Pal Saghon Dhungkar Choezom Monastery. It was as remote as it gets, the extreme wild west of Nepal just on the border with Tibet.

There was not much time to don our parachutes. I had not parachuted before; I had done the training, but both days the winds were too high and they did not allow us to jump. So my first jump would be in the high Himalaya. Devi had jumped before with her dad when they climbed unclimbed peaks in inaccessible regions. We put on the main chute and the auxiliary chutes, checked the rip cords, and checked each other to be sure we had the harnesses on correctly.

"We are going to have to use the control lines to navigate to one of the few flat landing sites in the area," said Devi.

Just one look down told me she did not need to overstate that. We were in the midst of mountains higher and larger than anything in North America.

"We're nearly over the drop zone, Colonel Lachhiman--those buildings down there at approximately 12,000 feet above sea level are Yalbang Monastery, so please circle and tell me when we are upwind and level at an altitude of 14,000 feet."

Mum was having trouble getting used to this new confidence in me. But she was controlling her fear. She gave me such a tight hug and said that I'd earned her confidence. Liam joined in on the hug, and then Devyani joined us, as did Devi.

"Someone has to pilot this plane," said Lachhiman.

"We love you, Colonel Lachhiman!" all of us shouted.

Colonel Lachhiman said, "We're approaching the drop zone, holding at 14,000 feet."

Devi and I broke away, put our hands on each other's shoulders, and made direct eye contact.

"Follow me down--see you in a few minutes on the ground," Devi said.

She opened the door under the wing and, without looking back, jumped. I followed her out the door and straightaway jumped. Later Mum told me that my not looking back was one of the hardest moments of her life, but that she understood I needed to stay focused.

Only a few moments later, Devi opened her 'chute, and I pulled the rip cord on my main chute. What a relief it was to see the canopy balloon open above me. After all those hours of instruction, telling you everything that can possibly go wrong gets you a bit paranoid. Fa said he preferred just basic instruction before diving or jumping, as you can relax to begin with and then learn more later--if you wish. It did seem an irresponsible and potentially fatal way to look at it, but, as I was learning, everyone's reasons are sufficient for them. It's what gives this world both its difficulties and variety. Fa would have loved to see this moment: Mum trusting me and allowing me to jump from a plane in the Himalayas on a sacred Quest.

CHAPTER FOUR
THRESHOLD GUARDIANS

Running into the Buddha

Then, there it was--in this unlikely moment and place, hurtling toward
a postage-stamp field surrounded by brightly coloured buildings--love, an
overwhelming feeling of love. I could not tell if it was coming from
below, above, or within. It felt like all three. I was surrounded by love. It
was like bliss. I was spellbound by this feeling for a few minutes, and
during this time, I'd forgotten to pull my control lines and follow Devi
upwind of the landing site. I pulled hard on the lines but I could see that I
would not make the small plateau-like field that was surrounded by steep
cliffs. Just as Devi landed adjacent to the buildings, I was directly over the
monastery and dropping quickly. There was a little courtyard in the centre
of the buildings; however, there was some kind of ceremony taking place
there. I had no choice. I steered for it as best I could and hit the ground
running but right in my path there was literally a big, golden . . . my last
word before hitting it was, "Buddddhhhaa!" I landed in the arms of a
huge, golden, smiling Buddha. It would have been better if it had been
softer. I slowly turned around to see my parachute float down and knock
off the hat of the High Lama and settle on those gathered around.

Rinpoche Pema Riksal carefully picked up his tall, red hat and put it
on his head. He nodded in my direction and waved for me to come over.
The students folded up my parachute very precisely as though it was
nothing more than a door or wall hanging and then made a space for me.

"Welcome. My name is Pema Riksal. What is yours?"

I was surprised to hear English spoken so clearly in this remote place.

"My name is Ray. I've been called Rashmi by the pilot--"

"Excellent. Ray it is. May I continue with my teaching?"

"Oh, yes, of course. Sorry for my interruption."

"Perhaps, Ati, you can sit beside our new student and translate."

"Hello, Ray," Ati whispered.

"Hello, Ati," I whispered back.

So Ati quietly translated the following teaching into my ear.

"If one has the habit of understanding suffering to be self-envisioned, we will thereby be able to make all occurrences of unwanted illness and suffering naturally dissolve.

I have noticed in many of you that even small external negative conditions snowball into a huge amount of additional suffering.

The cause of this is grasping and a crisis of impatience. In the West, we have heard of their preoccupation with 'drop-in': drop-in centres, drive by, instant this and that. Instant enlightenment without discipline and patience. Now, even here in Nepal, we have *Dharma Drop-in*."

The Rinpoche looked right at me. I think I went white as a sheet. Then a big smile lit up his face and he said, "This is funny, no?"

We all began to look at each other while laughing, smiling, and nodding our heads in agreement.

"Always good to remember," said Lama Pema Riksal, "*to lighten up while enlightening up.*

"Do not be annoyed by interruptions, they are an opportunity for something more real to take place. One-pointedness is deeper than what is happening on the surface. Take a look within; did you experience frustration that we were interrupted or did you feel curiosity? Often we do not recognize the Buddha on our path. Not often will it be like our friend Ray who actually runs into what is unmistakably the Buddha."

More laughs all around. Ati was now giggling, and I was missing parts of the translation.

I told Ati, "Stop giggling." But this made her giggle even harder.

"Cultivate curiosity . . ." was all I got from Ati, who was not able to speak without the giggling starting again.

I would have been more amused but I really did want to hear the teachings. So I started to look around at the well-maintained buildings. Then my gaze wandered to the other adepts. Then, near the front, I could see that there was what looked like a Western woman dressed in Nepalese clothing. It was Marie-Madeleine! At that moment, she caught my eye and winked at me and gestured that I should come and sit beside her.

I whispered my thanks to Ati, which set off another spasm of giggling.

Making my way through the tightly knit group, I sat down beside Marie-Madeleine. People shuffled around to make space for me. I felt uncomfortable causing more interruptions but I was SO pleased to have reconnected. I guess it was not so surprising, as this was one of the two closest monasteries to what I hoped would be Shambhala.

Marie-Madeleine and I did a long sitting hug. When we were finished, I was aware of the silence around me. Lama Pema Riksal was looking at me, smiling.

"Was this an unexpected meeting, Ray?" asked the Lama.

"Yes, we had not agreed on a location."

"Lama Marie-Madeleine, was this an unexpected meeting?"

"Ray is correct--we did not plan on an exact meeting place. However, our meeting was not a surprise to me."

"Ah, here we have two different views. Which is the right view?"

There was some enthusiastic debate that I could not understand. Then Marie-Madeleine translated the Lama Pema Riksal's response.

"Awakening of intrinsic awareness (*rigpa*), the innate nature of the mind as it is, leads to the realization of the Great Perfection. This is the great secret of mind. Just as Ray and Lama Marie-Madeleine are part of the Great Perfection, so are each of you here in this moment part of the Great Perfection--this is the right view. Dzogchen is the path to this realization."

Lama Pema Riksal picked up his *vajra* and bell and recited a mantra to end the teaching.

I was starting to wonder where Devi was. As I was getting up to leave, Marie-Madeleine pulled me down.

"You don't leave before the Rinpoche leaves."

"I thought this was a musical interlude," I whispered back.

Marie-Madeleine gave me one of those wry smiles that I became so fond of.

After thanking the Rinpoche for his teaching, I left Marie-Madeleine and went to look for Devi outside the courtyard. Her chute was already packed into her backpack and left in the clearing. Perhaps she went to the kitchen to get some food . . . or knows someone at the monastery? I suppose anything's possible--especially with Devi. I just reminded myself that I'd seen her land safely.

Marie-Madeleine invited me into her sweet little hermitage, as it had an extra cot. We had the most marvelous view of the hills in the foreground and the towering, snow-capped peaks behind. I decided this was a good place to wait for Devi's return. The place was picturesque, the hermitage was warm, the head Lama had a sense of humour, and I was really wanting to get to know Marie-Madeleine and hear her stories about Alexandra David-Neel.

That evening, Devi still had not returned, so I checked out her parachute pack and inside was a note:

"Dear Ray, sorry for leaving so quickly, but there's trouble in paradise and I knew that you'd be in good hands here. I think you'll find the delay fortuitous. I'll be back as soon as possible and we'll head to Shambhala together--with Love, Devi."

I was concerned about the "trouble in paradise" bit, but it was good to know that Devi did not just disappear. So I decided the best thing was to relax into the routine of the monastery. After a silent dinner, Marie-Madeleine and I returned to her hermitage and she stoked the peat fire and made me some English tea with goat's milk and honey. We sat around the fire and let the deep peace settle in. It was a rare evening when there was not a persistent wind. In the distance, there were bells chiming and the deep chanting of the monks and nuns. Marie-Madeleine threw a few sticks on to bring the fire up and give it that inviting crackle.

Meeting the Adventurer of All Realms

"Please," I asked, "tell me your story and how you met Alexandra David-Neel. I've got her *Magic and Mysticism in Tibet,* so I know some of her stories. Honestly, I'm more interested in your story, how you came to be a caregiver, as I'm at a crossroads in my life and not sure what to do next."

"That's a good, honest place to be. I'll do my best, as I, too, consider myself to be a storyteller, although not one who tells much or often; but I believe it's important to share the patterns of our lives as inspiration for others.

"I was a sensitive child, and there was a lot of drama in my childhood. My mother was on a journey of unconditional love, and my father was badly wounded. My mother tried to keep loving us all and not abandon anyone. It seemed impossible. Out of that a lot of fears grew. Fear of my marrying someone who would turn out to be like my father, fear of subjecting children to the drama I had experienced, fear of having a child taken away by violence. Fear, fear, fear. These fears controlled me. All my arguments sounded rational, but they kept me to the sidelines of life-- many suitors but unmarried. I played it safe, as I knew how dangerous this river of life could be. I had relationships only with men who really were not available for one reason or other. Nothing was going to sweep me away. Then, during a fling with a married man, I got pregnant. I decided to keep the child. The boy was my love child.

"To keep the story short, I did everything I could for Daniel. I gave him all the love that was stored up inside me, I loved him unconditionally. I pursued my spiritual work. I studied at night to become a psychotherapist and also to become a better, more conscious parent. But perhaps as I was often a single parent, I could not do it all myself. He got taunted and beaten in the schoolyard but he did not want to let me know what a hard time he was having.

"When he was in his teens, on a day that I will forever remember in near-infinite detail, I came home, and he was in his room, not breathing. There was a spoon with white powder beside his bed. I called the ambulance. I told the paramedics that he could not die, that I could not live without my beautiful boy. I pleaded and raved and went mad with grief when they pronounced him dead at the hospital. All my worst fears had become true.

"I could not live with this emptiness inside, with this lack of meaning, without his voice and kind words. Somehow I got through the worst year of my life and then decided the best way through was to write the rest of his story, to write out the adventures that he did not get to live. *Paris will help me do this*, I thought. It was during this time that I first saw Alexandra David-Neel. The writing was beginning to help me to feel again, and my curiosity was returning. While on my daily walk from Montmartre to Pigalle, I saw an old woman sitting with a tattooed and pierced group of teens in a back alley. I had seen her a few times, out in all weather, often in unusual situations. Then it came into my mind, this was a woman who was fearless. How did she become fearless? I was determined to find a way to meet her.

"The opportunity came a few days later when I ended up behind her in a line at the local health-food store checkout. As it happens, there was a small scene: She had left her handbag at home and had no way to pay. She was insisting that she should restock all the food so the store would not be punished for her oversight. That's when I seized the moment and offered to pay. Alexandra looked me over, graciously accepted, then insisted that I walk with her so she could serve me tea and pay me back in full. That was our first meeting. Later I found out it was one of her many techniques of meeting "like-minded" people.

"I sensed someone who was completely real, completely herself, and she loved people openly and fearlessly. This old woman had somehow found her way through some of the big questions to ways of being in the world that engaged my curiosity. From that moment forward, our friendship helped invigorate my writing. In some ways, I was not just writing but *being written*. I was drawn to visit and spend more time with Alexandra.

"I once took her on a short morning hike along the River Seine and that's when I discovered how much she still loved adventures. But it was also becoming clearer that she could not manage on her own. I suspected dementia, but it was atypical, perhaps because of her strong spiritual life and inner resources. Over the next six months, it became more and more clear that she could not live alone. Then one day when she was out shopping alone, she fell. I was supposed to meet her that afternoon and I got a call from the hospital that Alexandra was not able to make our appointment. I raced over to the hospital; her face, her shoulder and her hip were black and blue, but somehow nothing was broken.

"I said, 'Alexandra, you had a bad fall today, but according to the doctors and the MRI, it looks like nothing's broken.'

"She said, 'Dear, it was only cement.'

"As though there were some substance that was much harder and more resilient than cement.

"In retrospect, it was a series of heart-opening moments, but that was a breaking point, so to speak. I offered to move in.

"'I'd love that,' Alexandra said. 'But if I ever become a burden just put me away and get on with your life.'

"Alexandra was so good and careful with my time, she did everything she could do, and more. And together, we went on more and more soft adventures, and I can honestly say she came back to life. We had difficulties, yes: Some of her relatives had me down for a money-grubber and taking advantage of an old woman."

"That's terrible," I added. "I can't believe that they would have seen you that way."

"When people are unconscious of their motivations, they create all sorts of illusions to make themselves feel better and rationalize pursuing their self-interest. People who are not motivated by love feel everyone else has ulterior motives and so they project their baser motives on others. It is a hard lesson to learn in life for people who are motivated by love.

"There is no way to be loving in this life without also being strong. Let's end here for tonight and enjoy some quiet time around the fire."

Grandsy and the Hudson's Bay Incident

Marie-Madeleine served us both some more tea that had been kept hot hanging over the fire. I started to see similarities between Grandsy and Alexandra David-Neel. Grandsy had lived on every continent and loved adventures; she was loving by nature and had amazing encounters with people on the Danforth and at the Bay Department store. One time she had just entered the Hudson's Bay Store and there was a commotion in one of the main aisles. There was a large group of people gathered around, and in the centre, two burly security guards were holding a person down on the ground with his arms behind his back. Grandsy looked at the man on the ground and for a moment he looked like Grandsy's eldest son, who was a university professor. Grandsy's eyesight was not the best, and street people and university professors do look very much alike. But it was that split-second moment of recognition that it could have been her son, which morphed into: well, it's *some* mother's son . . . and that made Grandsy act.

She pushed her way through the crowd and asked the pinned-down man, "Would you prefer ME to escort you out of the store?" He nodded his head vigorously. Mum looked at the security guards and said, "I'll pay for whatever he has taken so I'm sure that your services are no longer required."

The crowd was murmuring their approval, and so the guards stepped back. Mum reached out with her hand, and the man got up and dusted himself off; then Mum offered him her arm, and quite formally they walked out of the Hudson's Bay Store.

Sitting there sipping warm tea, I recalled how often I'd visit Grandsy and tell her everything that was going on in my life, and she'd respond enthusiastically; then there'd be a pause, and sometimes I'd ask, "How did *your* day go, Grandsy? Did anything happen on the Danforth or at the Bay?" And she'd tell me some amazing little gem of a story about what had happened that very day. How many stories are lost because no one is there to ask? But I guess they were not lost, as other people were perhaps telling them. Those stories that Grandsy told me washed over me; they had travelled with me all the way across the world.

The Right Stuff

The next morning, Devi still had not returned. I went looking about the monastery. There were so many beautiful carvings and tapestries. It was such a feast of images, but as there was no central heating, I got a chill. I have no idea how people meditated here. So I made my way to the kitchen where a nun whose name was Chokyi was showing a group of novices how to prepare meals. When I came in, Chokyi right away noticed that I was cold and brought out a little stool and put it near the hearth. She brought me a steaming mug of tea. I clutched my hands around it and nodded appreciatively. But when I sipped it I nearly spit it out. How could I tell Chokyi that the milk was sour and the tea salty? I looked around and everyone else was merrily drinking the tea. That's when I realized they liked it this way. I drank it down quickly to get the warmth and to not taste it. Chokyi nodded her approval and immediate filled my mug up again. This one I drank more slowly. Chokyi would come over and just stroke my hair or give me fresh tidbits of food. I felt loved in that kitchen. Later I found out she was the reincarnation of a high female Lama whose path in this lifetime was loving service.

When I was good and warm and filled with food, I thought I'd wander out to the courtyard to see what time the teaching started. Novices and monks were just gathering, and so I sat down contentedly. The air was cool but the sun was shining. To our north were lined soaring after soaring peak on a scale that boggled the mind. To the south stretched purple rolling hills as far as the eye could see. This was indeed a bigger reality, a tall tale.

As Lama Pema Riksal wove his way through the cross-legged bodies to the dais, he tripped over my outstretched leg. Quick as a flash, several novices leapt up and caught him. With their help, he made his way unsteadily to the cushion. The novices were solicitous, but as soon as he was seated, he shushed them away with his hands and began a few minutes of chanting. I felt guilty that I nearly tripped the old Lama. What if he had fallen and hurt himself? I was feeling really bad when I heard a voice. I looked around, but no one was speaking to me, and the old monk was still chanting.

I closed my eyes and listened again. "Ray, it was just an old man playing a trick on you. Look at what your mind is creating! Welcome to the teaching."

Freaked, I opened my eyes, and Lama Riksal stopped chanting and winked at me.

"Now let's begin our lesson for the day, shall we?" said Lama Pema Riksal.

"Our minds are like a room. Take a look at the physical rooms you occupy: Are they full of stuff, are they messy, or are they neat and clean? This is just an indication, a result--not the cause. You can keep tidying your room but if you do not deal with the cause, it just becomes messy right away--correct?"

We all murmured, "Correct."

"The mind is the most important room. You must first know what is in it, how to tidy it, and, most important, how to empty it. Most minds that come here are cluttered, and all we do here at the monastery is teach you how to empty it. Correct?"

We all murmured, "Correct."

"Not correct. We teach you that there are no walls, that there is no room. But that's a more advanced teaching. For now, there is a room. First you must discover just how much is in that room. That is the beginning of meditation. To see just how crowded your room is. Parents arguing and criticizing, little wounded child constantly blubbering and complaining. Your whole family is crammed in, and every little beep and reference to yourself on what is called the World Wide Web. Which now extends even to this remote place."

I could see the Lama was referring to me directly. He obviously had knowledge of the West and global trends, as I did not see monks walking around with cellphones "liking" each other's meditation pages.

"Why do we keep wanting to shove more things into an already full room?"

I was just about to offer the first thing that came to my mind and then I realized that I'd done this many times before in Mrs. Macfiercesome's class and she took pains to point out what a rhetorical question was. So I caught myself.

"Because we feel empty inside. And we feel empty inside because we're filling it with the wrong stuff."

I felt like this was an opportunity for call and response so I called out, "What's the right stuff?"

The old Rinpoche livened up and said, "You've seen that one too, good movie. Maybe next lifetime I will be more like your Tom Cruise."

Everyone nodded and laughed. I guess along with the World Wide Web, that movie had made it all the way here.

"Tom Cruise had the right stuff--do *you* have the right stuff?" asked the Lama.

I thought, *that crafty old Rinpoche does not miss a beat.*

"I can't tell you what should be in your room. Well, you novices I can. What should be in your increasingly empty rooms is your Yidams. For many of you that is Arya Tara or Jetzen Drolma; for Catholics, it's the Divine Mother or the Blessed Virgin Mary; for the others, you must find someone or something to put in your room, to believe in. At this stage, an empty room will become inhabited by demonic forces. Now I am going to ask all of you to visualize your room and see what is in the centre of it."

The Centre of My Room

The Lama picked up his prayer wheel and *vajra*/thunderbolt and chanted for a few moments. I closed my eyes to better visualize, but I could not see anything in the middle of the room. Things were crowded around the outside of the room, but nothing was in the centre. I got scared. Then I heard my name. "Ray, Ray." Was it coming from inside my head? No, it was the Lama, calling me out loud.

"Ray, what is in the centre of your room?"

Oh, my goodness, I was being put on the spot and I couldn't see anything in my room! I couldn't speak. I stuttered and reached for my throat. Then I felt them. That morning I had put on the pearls Grandsy had given me just before going on this trip. She had worn them every day of her adult life and she said they would keep me safe.

I was just about to say, "Grandsy" . . . then I remembered the story of Ganesh and the Pearl of Great Price, a story Grandsy had often told me as a child. Grandsy had been born in 1919, in Darjeeling--the foothills of these very mountains, the Himalayas. This story must have been told to her by her nanny.

Ganesh and the Pearl of Great Price

When he was a young elephant, his mother had told him stories of Hindustan. He would say, "Mummy, tell me that story, that story about Ganesh, you know the one--tell it, tell it, please." And she would, over and over again and so eventually he learned it word for word. He would never let her miss a word; or, if she changed one, he'd correct her. She never refused him the story. She knew that one day, when he really needed it most, he would understand what the story really meant.

Surrounded by the tallest mountains in the world, hidden deep in the heart of the Himalayan Mountains lay the Kingdom of Hindustan. When the sun rose over Hindustan, each of the peaks that surrounded the valley lit up like matchsticks. It was as though a circle of fire surrounded the kingdom. As the sun rose higher, each of those snow-capped peaks shone like jewels in a king's crown. And the wearer of that crown, the King of Hindustan, was the fairest, kindest man that ever was. His name was King Ibrahim ben Adham (may his tribe increase). The king had ruled this hidden kingdom for many years and now that he was getting old he was looking for someone to replace him.

There was also a mystery: A pearl was missing from the king's crown, and ever since it had been lost, one of the mountain peaks did not light up with the sun; it became known as the Black Mountain. At the same time, there was great fear in Hindustan because of a fearsome tiger living in the mountains, who on nights of the full moon, would come down and drag the inhabitants of Hindustan back into his cave and devour them.

Ganesh was a young elephant. He seemed to be the only one in the kingdom who didn't seem to care about finding the pearl or being king. Instead, he set out toward the mountains to find the tiger. After many days of travelling, he came to where the tiger tracks ended: a cave in the Dark Mountain. Ganesh lay his trunk down in front of the cave like a snake and waited. That night, the sound of crunching bones was so loud that Ganesh became afraid; but still he waited.

At first light, the tiger put his head out of the cave and saw a snake lying there. *What luck!* he thought. The tiger leapt on it and tore into it with its claws and began dragging it back into its cave. But it was attached to an elephant. Although Ganesh was in great pain, he rolled up the tiger in his trunk and squeezed so hard that the tiger promised not to attack the people anymore.

On his way down the mountain, he noticed that one of the tiger's eyes was weeping. He asked what the problem was. The tiger replied that something had lodged in his eye many years ago and when he could not remove it, he became very angry. Ganesh put his trunk over the tiger's eye and gently sucked. Plunk, out came a small object. It was a pearl.

When Ganesh returned, the king called a holiday, and all the people gathered to celebrate him and the now peaceful tiger. Ganesh presented the missing pearl to the King. The pearl fit perfectly into the centre of the crown. The moment it was placed there, the Black Mountain was transformed into a shining beacon. The king said, you have found the Pearl of Great Price and you have had the courage to pluck to it from the eye of a tiger--you are surely our new king.

And so that is why from that day to this, elephants all across Asia have a pearl placed in their foreheads to remind them that with all their strength they must never forget to be kind.

Many years passed, the young elephant's mother had long since died, and he had travelled all over India, Pakistan, and far into the Himalayas building roads and clearing forests for plantations. Wherever he went he told the story of Ganesh, till it was a part of him. Whenever he faced hardship and fear, he knew that eventually he would reach Hindustan, and this thought gave him peace.

Eventually, he became too old for such work, and so his owners decided to send him to the zoo in Karachi. As he walked up the ramp onto the truck it struck him: He was never going to Hindustan.

It was at this very same moment Ganesh realized what his mother was telling him as a boy: He already had the Pearl of Great Price in his own heart, and Hindustan was within.

All this came back to me as I touched those pearls and I knew the answer to what was in the centre of my room.

"It's the Pearl of Great Price!" I cried out.

"Are you sure it's not a pile of dirty laundry?"

Fa had taught me with native elders to never be offended, to laugh especially loudly at all jokes about you. It is not meant to be cruel.

"Well, maybe the Pearl is buried under a few clothes," I admitted.

Everyone laughed along with the Lama, as he chuckled out loud, "Pearl buried under dirty laundry."

I had to admit it was a pretty good one, and as I laughed I realized that the laughter was not scorn but love; there was this timbre to the laughter that pointed to the humorous reality of life, the everyday paradoxes, the mundane and the highly spiritual that were there literally on top of each other. As I reflected on this, I found it more and more funny. I looked over at Marie-Madeleine, and she was on the edge of splitting a seam and that put us both over and I just lost it right there. I guffawed, I snorted, I rolled onto the monk beside me, tears streaming down my face. I totally lost it. I looked over at Marie-Madeleine and she was rolling with laughter and now everyone else was, including the Lama, who needed to hang on to his tall Red Hat.

As the laughter eventually began to die down, the Lama did a ritual with the prayer wheel, the *vajra*, and a drum that had two shells tied to it, so when he twisted it back and forth it made a very regular and trance-like beat. He asked us to spend some time visualizing and listening to the Yidam in the centre of our room.

My mind wandered a bit. I was thinking, *I could really do a year of this; this should be Grade 13*. A year of meditation, mindfulness, and self-awareness . . . an exchange program with monks. I could handle it, except for the lack of central heating. My room quickly became filled with thoughts about me, me, me. So I tried for a while to let those go, watch them arise and not follow them, arise and not follow, arise and not follow, over and over again until there was a little time and space to spend with my Pearl.

I was pretty chilled by the time Lama Riksal stopped chanting. This time he shooed everyone out of the courtyard with his hands, then he pointed at me and said, "You stay."

The Lama beckoned me to come close.

"You look cold again, Ray."

"Yes, Lama," I said through chattering teeth. "My Fa taught me to swim in cold water and not panic but I find it cold here away from central heating."

"Oh, ho ho, we in Nepal and Tibet have true central heating, it is called *tum-mo*. I will show you tonight and extend your Fa's teaching so you can stay warm not only in cold water but in air.

"Now you go see High Kitchen Lama."

I nodded vigorously and attempted to get up calmly but as I got halfway across the courtyard, I started to run toward the kitchen. My little stool was right there beside the cook stove, which was glowing with beautiful, radiant heat. There was a pot of water boiling on the hob, and Chokyi was mixing in herbs. Moments later, she poured me a cup. I took a small sip, as I was worried that it was going to be like that salty, rancid, yak butter tea I had yesterday. But this was marvellous, full of wild herbs that I'd never tasted before, and sweet. I took a few more quick sips and blew into the cup. The aroma enveloped me. Chokyi looked down at me lovingly, and I looked up at her with gratitude. She stroked my hair and made this kind of contented clucking. Minutes later, out of a steaming pot she pulled *momo*s, Tibetan dumplings. Dumplings were Grandsy's and my favourite food, and oh, my, were they delicious! Maybe this *tum-mo* was something like the *momo*s, which certainly heated me up from the inside.

I wanted to get back to Marie-Madeleine's hermitage to hear more of her caregiving story before this *tum-mo* started.

When I got to the hermitage, Marie-Madeleine was cleaning off the eye shadow that had streaked from all the laughing. More tea was on the hob; I was going to get a champion bladder from all this tea-drinking. Marie-Madeleine told me that Nepalis and Tibetans were the biggest tea drinkers in the world, far out-drinking the British or the Chinese. On average, one kilo per month. It's almost Tibet's biggest import. I loved it. It was another thing that warmed you from the inside.

Becoming the Medicine

As Marie-Madeleine and I sat across from each other, beside her little hearth, holding each other's outstretched hands, looking directly into each other's eyes, it was a feeling of connection, fondness, and love; that, too, warmed me from the inside.

"Tell me more of your story," I asked.

"My story would take many, many more days to tell."

"Tell it, then. I'll take the time; I'll stay here."

"That's good of you to say, but you've got more adventures on your Quest and more to learn from others. If you want to learn more, there's a book by Verity Jenkins called the *Caregiver's Dilemma*. In a narrative format, he shows how to create holistic care for a loved one.

"But there are a few lessons I'd like to share--if you've got the patience?"

"I'm all ears; this is exactly what I came all this way to learn. I'll keep the book in mind. Do tell more . . ."

The wind was picking up; I could hear great gusts roaring up and down the mountain, pounding the little hermitage that was clinging to the cliffside. It was the best place in the world to hear a story.

"Ray, you're a storyteller, and you have the Pearl of Great Price. The medicine that you carry is to combine these two gifts. You can heal your Grandsy through narrative."

"What? Wait a minute. I can't heal Alzheimer's with stories!"

"Oh dear, yes, I am sorry, I thought as much. And I suppose Alexandra David-Neel had something of the sort."

"Something of the sort?"

"Yes, my dear; there are many kinds of dementia. We're at the very beginning stages of understanding the various types, and they are not easy to differentiate between without an autopsy, which does not help the living. And we are only just discovering the profound impact of nature, exercise, adventure, holistic care, and, most important, a person's unique spiritual journey in the progression of Alzheimer's/dementia.

"So I say 'something of the sort' because although we can learn a lot from science, it is very much focused on medication to solve problems, such as preventing hallucinations in dementia. They are fulfilling our desire to create a pill to solve our elders' problems, so we can get on with our own lives. Whereas holistic care requires time, commitment, kindness, and knowledge; it requires setting aside your personal goals and objectives for a time to walk alongside others. These traditional skills are largely invisible to science.

"One problem is that we see caregiving as a one-way street. The elder is receiving all the care. What is hidden is that if you are looking after a true elder, not a bitter old person, that elder will transform themselves into your medicine. That is very important to know and begin to see. If it's not happening, perhaps you aren't really seeing the nature of the exchange, or you are not coming from a perspective of gratitude, or the elder is a 'hungry ghost,' as they say here in Tibet. If your elder is someone who you know in your heart would do anything for you and you'd do anything for them, you know for sure that caring for them is the right thing. If you perceive that an elder has given more in their life than they have received, then caring for them is likely the right thing."

"That sounds just like Grandsy," I replied. "She had a very difficult life with Grandfa; he was forty-five when she married him, and she was nineteen and fresh out of convent school. Grandfa was dashing, daring, and adventurous. He had gone from racing motorcycles and running contraband by boat from England to war-torn France to medical school to becoming a hero by walking through a minefield to rescue an injured man. Even though everyone warned her about Grandfa, she was in love.

"Grandsy wanted to create a family and have children to love. Grandfa wanted adventure and he loved surgery. Both in extremes. After an early first child, Grandfa didn't want any more. The difficult truth is that Grandfa ended Grandsy's pregnancies for the next eighteen years.

"By then she had become strong and determined enough to keep Fa and his sister. Soon after that, Grandfa got himself kicked out of Australia, joined a cult, became an alcoholic, got into firearms and hunting, gave up surgery, and became a psychiatrist--something that he was wholly unsuited for. According to Fa, this combination of things released what the old Europeans and Tibetans would call 'demonic forces.'

"Those stories are for Fa to tell . . . I know there are many dark ones he did not tell me. All I know is that Grandfa nearly killed his family many times, and Grandsy was caught between keeping her children safe and trying to save the man she loved. And she did--she loved her children wholeheartedly and ultimately kept them safe. Eventually, Grandfa became an unruly but gentle old man, who she continued to care for right up to his death a few years ago.

"Now she was truly free for the first time in her life--and she had Alzheimer's. IT WAS NOT FAIR!"

"That is a profound motivation for caring. To bring what we see as justice to this life. You will need that fire on this journey.

"But there is a subtle and perhaps a more profound reason for making this choice. All spiritual paths, all religions, all routes and ridges lead to a single summit and that summit is unconditional love--it is of course the Pearl of Great Price. Many do not learn it in this lifetime. For many it takes many, many lifetimes to learn. We may get tastes of it with our children, or with pets. But to be in a relationship with a true master of unconditional love is the greatest blessing of multiple lifetimes. You can save many lifetimes of struggle by Apprenticing in Love in this lifetime.

"Your storytelling plays a key role in this. Your Grandsy needs meaning to complete her journey. To her, if someone she loves truly needs what she has to offer, she will climb any mountain, even Mt. Alzheimer's and Mt. Dementia. You are the keeper of her story, you keep telling her stories of the hero that she truly is and she will be both the teacher and the wise elder even as she becomes a child again. What will happen is that a spiral of love will wrap itself around you both, and together you will become invincible. You will walk though fire, you will walk on water, you will move mountains; miracles will become like pebbles on your path, and you will come to know love like you have never imagined it. And this I know, because I've lived it."

I looked over at Marie-Madeleine, and she was absolutely radiant. She believed what she was saying, and I believed her.

But I had no time to reflect on this--the door burst open and with a blast of cold air Devi swooped in. I ran over and we hugged, but underneath the layers of clothing I sensed her body was as tense as steel. I pulled away to look into her face, and her eyes were glowing.

"The nuns have tricked me. Where I was taking you was remarkable but was not the real entrance to Shambhala. I've found the real entrance and I've come back to get you so we can go together."

I was worried about Devi's intensity, and she was ignoring Marie-Madeleine.

"The real entrance to Shambhala? What were you doing there, young lady?" interjected Marie-Madeleine in a very stern tone.

Devi swung around and said, "And who might you be?"

"I am one of the keepers of Shambhala." Delivered in a voice that seemed so much bigger than Marie-Madeleine and somehow ancient.

We both were shocked.

Devi snapped out of it and in a calmer voice replied, "Well, at least I *think* it's the right entrance. I discovered that the nuns who use the Shambhala Trekking Agency as a front tricked me into believing a ceremonial Honey Hunters' cave was the entrance to Shambhala--then employed me to take Ray to the false entrance."

"Perhaps there are two entrances; perhaps there are many," replied Marie-Madeleine.

"Oh I'm not going to be tricked by words any longer," responded Devi.

"That's a good intention, hold on to it, dear, but you've got a lot of life ahead of you. However for the moment let us participate in the *tum-mo* competition."

I was a bit confused. "The Lama told me it was a spiritual practice."

"Yes, it is," replied Marie-Madeleine; "adepts practise *tum-mo* throughout the year, and from time to time, on the full moon, they hold competitions on the glacier above."

"A spiritual practice as a competition--that's interesting. Are you familiar with *tum-mo*, Devi?" I asked.

"I certainly am, but I'd far rather be on my way to Shambhala with all haste. I suppose I can wait till the morning. Especially since it seems that your friend Marie-Madeleine knows something about Shambhala."

"Marie-Madeleine is an amazing woman, with a most remarkable story; you should have been properly introduced to her when you burst into her hermitage," I stated with mock sternness.

"Apologies for my behaviour, Marie-Madeleine," said Devi.

"Among other things," I said, "Marie-Madeleine was the caregiver for Alexandra David-Neel."

"NO WAY! WOW, how amazing that must have been . . . The greatest woman explorer of all the realms. I bow at your feet and offer my most profound apologies again."

"Oh, dear, there's no need for that! No offence was taken, so no apology is needed. However I do sense we've got some interesting times ahead together."

"Really?" said Devi.

"Really," replied Marie-Madeleine.

"What about me?" I asked.

"In your heart you know what you must do, and it will be far beyond your expectations."

"What about me?" asked Devi.

"Devi, you will achieve in a short time what you came here for. That is a life gift rarely given to people."

"How do you know this?" I asked.

"When we see something difficult all the way through--when we sacrifice for others--one of the gifts we receive is Second Sight. It's not the time to talk about it, but there will come a time when you wonder how you know certain things.

"But for now, let's us girls go and rock those spiritual games and knock a few monks off their towels."

I had no idea what that meant, but Devi evidently did, and together we roused a cheer.

"Into your bathing suits, ladies," said Marie-Madeleine. "I will line us up some big woollen coats to wear as we climb up."

Bathing suits? We're at 15,000 feet . . . there's only glaciers and huge mountains above us!

"Oh," said Devi, "Ray, my friend, you are in for a big surprise tonight. Remember our first day together?"

"Of course I do--how could I forget! You nearly killed us."

"Well, strap on your bikini, we're going to take another dragon out for a wild ride--a competition that Westerners never get to see," said Devi with a mischievous grin.

Ouch, this was shaping up to be more than some regular night party on the beach. It was perhaps payback time from the Universe for lying about Mum's pink bikini.

We all changed into our bathing suits, and Marie-Madeleine opened a big closet and inside were three beautiful, heavy, white yak wool jackets. We donned them.

Marie-Madeleine looked over at Devi and me mischievously. "You, my dears, are going to give those monks and some of those nuns something to meditate on."

Devi smiled, but I said, "What do you mean?"

"In the Vajrayana tradition, to overcome desire, the nuns and monks are taught to see the object of their desire as a rotting corpse at various stages of decomposition."

Ew. That was not welcome information.

Marie-Madeleine pulled out an old, unlabelled bottle. "It's local *raksi*;

it'll warm your cockles."

Devi said, "If tomorrow we'll be seen as corpses in some monk's fantasy, let's raise our glasses to tonight. 'All cares to the wind we merrily fling, for the damp cold grave is a dead sure thing, but it's a dead sure thing that we're alive tonight and that damp cold grave is out of sight!'"

We threw back the *raksi*; it shot through my whole digestive tract like liquid fire.

We all hollered together, even Marie-Madeleine. "Let's go kick some Tibetan monks' ass!"

I was warming up to these spiritual competitions.

A Question for the Bon Shaman

The *rag-dungs*--those great big Tibetan long horns whose sounds bellow, roar, burble, rumble, and purr down long, high-mountain valleys-- started to peal from around the monastery's walls. The ceremony was beginning. Devi winked at Marie-Madeleine and grabbed the big bottle of *raksi* and tucked it into her yak coat.

We arrived at the courtyard and were greeted by a scene that could not have been more opposite to the past couple of days. Big torches lit up the courtyard. Drums were being beaten loudly. Elaborate costumes and masks with the most gruesome features were dancing wildly around a central fire. It looked like the stage was set for a Dante-esque drama.

"What's going on?" I asked Marie-Madeleine

"About one thousand years ago, Padmasambhava was reportedly the first Buddhist to arrive in Nepal and Tibet. He fought mythical spiritual battles with the indigenous shamans of Nepal and Tibet, the Bon Pos. These Bon-Po shamans represented the earth spirits and are closely related to the Siberian shamans, which may have been the source of shamanic practices worldwide."

I remembered some pretty graphic descriptions of Bon Po rituals in *Magic and Mystery in Tibet*.

"But these people are Buddhist-- they are peaceful and mostly vegetarian. It seems so out of place."

"What Padmasambhava cleverly did was to integrate the wrathful deities that were being exorcised by the Bon Pos into new visualizations and meditative practices. He co-opted these wrathful deities and transformed their vampire-like natures into protectors of the most beautiful aspects of our spiritual nature. But he did not completely defeat them. He left a small opening where the Bon Pos are called upon as part of highly ritualized ceremonies where the old earth spirits are tamed by recent incarnations of Padmasambhava all over again."

"Wow, did the Bon Pos agree to this?"

"Mostly, yes, as it gives them the freedom to practise their old ways without interference, and a venue at various Buddhist ceremonies.

"But," Marie-Madeleine went on to say, "it is also more than that. The Bon Pos believe that there must be harmony and balance between the humans and the earth spirits. To them, all human and animal illness, plagues, crop failures, and extreme weather are caused by a lack of harmony and imbalance between the human and natural world."

"How can you disagree with this perspective?" I said. "Especially since we've ignored this imbalance, and it is becoming more and more costly and difficult to maintain. Asthma, cancer, and extreme weather are caused by us obviously ignoring a basic truth that these shamans have known since the beginning of human history."

Still, as rational and obvious as this all sounded, I was not prepared for what took place. I was told this was a practitioner of "White Bon," so I knew that they weren't going to bring out a deer and kill it ritualistically. The Bon practitioner was in stark contrast to the colourful Tibetan Buddhist dancers and wrathful spirits. It looked like he was dressed in old skins and had a huge number of cloth strips hanging from him. It gave him a Yeti-like appearance. Also, he carried a large number of ritual objects attached to his waist and was holding what looked exactly like a native drum and drumstick--festooned with feathers. The slow-moving masked dancers with their precise movements surrounded the shaman, while in contrast he became more and more animated and ecstatic. Clearly, he was moving into a trance.

"You see those three mirrors on his altar? Through the top of his skull, the last place to close up on a newborn, these mirrors are gateways that give his spirit access to the celestial realm (Lha); the earth and mountain realm (Tsen); and the subterranean and watery realms (Lu). While the shaman is hunting out where the imbalance is, his body is temporarily inhabited by a *pawo* or spirit guide that can answer your questions."

"I have a question! I must ask him about Fa."

"Be careful, Ray. If you attract the shaman, he will not just tell you what you want to hear, he will journey into the three realms, and you can't be sure what he'll bring back."

At that moment, the shaman had moved over to a very handsome monk who was lying on the ground. After dancing around him and chanting in a wildly strange voice that included what was clearly laughter, he pulled out a bone knife and plunged it into the side of the young monk. Even though there appeared to be blood everywhere, the monk made no sound. Then the shaman reached into the wound in the monk's side and pulled out a lump of ice. Moments later, the monk was being pulled to his feet, and, although he was staggering, he was encouraged to dance.

I know that sounds preposterous and clearly staged, but you had to be there to feel the impact and the truth of it. I felt the personal truth of it strike home.

Devi whispered, "Narcissism is not just a Western phenomenon; it covers your heart like ice."

I couldn't stand knowing that I hadn't asked the shaman about Fa-- just in case.

"What do I do to ask the shaman a question?"

"You simply lie down."

"Are you sure, Ray?"

"Go for it, Ray," said Devi.

One of the hardest things I had to do on this trip was to lie down. I didn't trust the Bon-Po shaman; they were not trying to be nice people; they were scary. But I had to try.

I fell to the ground and lay there quite a while before I started to hear the drum get louder. Soon that's all I heard.

Then a voice came through clear as a bell. "What's your question?"

"Where is my father?" I spoke through tears.

I have never seen leaps like that, in a flash the shaman was through the mirrors; he danced and flew and swam and tunnelled through what seemed like infinite realms. All the while, the drum was flying with him. I lost track of time . . . I watched him and, in a sense, I travelled with him. No doubt he was going to places in my memory and perhaps the memory of Fa. Who really knows? But to witness it, I was left with no doubt that an epic journey was taking place.

Then I heard a voice in my ear. "There is a door."

"An actual door, or a metaphorical door?" I asked with some ferocity, as I was tired of clues. Fa left a trail of metaphors, which like bread crumbs are hard to follow.

Then the same voice said, "An actual door."

"Where?" I grew excited.

I became aware that there was a monk translating between the shaman and me.

"Near the top of a mountain."

"What mountain?"

"Gang Rinpoche"

"What is Gang Rinpoche?"

The monk whispered, "'Rinpoche' usually refers to an enlightened teacher but it literally means, 'precious one, jewel.' 'Gang' in Tibetan means 'the place of four rivers.'"

"So the mountain with the door is referred to as the Precious Jewel of Four Rivers."

"Yes, also called Guru Mountain, a teacher mountain."

"Is it an actual place, a real mountain, or is it just something you visualize?"

"Both."

"So there's a real door on an actual mountain?" I had to be sure with these Tibetans.

"Yes. In the West, this mountain is known as Mount Kailash."

"Fa went there!" I replied. "It was one of his favourite places on earth!"

The monk replied, "Ray, all the Shaman is saying is that he has followed him and seen him go through the door on the Holy Mountain."

"Okay, okay, that's more than the RCMP discovered."

The shaman says that he has one more thing for you. In his travelling to the lower world, he saw that you were in a very sweet cave beside a river. He recognizes that cave. He can take you there."

"Please thank the Shaman for me."

Then, at the last minute, I realized that I needed to offer something in exchange.

"Is there anything I can give the shaman in exchange?"

"He says he likes your yak coat."

"I can't give him my coat--all I've got on under it is my bathing suit."

"He doesn't know what a bathing suit is. But he can lend you his coat to take to the *tum-mo*."

Oh, GOD NO! His coat was stained with old blood, and I'm sure that every kind of insect was just hovering in it trying to keep themselves warm. So much so that to my mind it created a kind of blur around the coat. These Bon Pos were also known not to wash for an entire season-- that was during the winter, mind you. But HOW COULD I REFUSE? He had travelled through worlds for me.

As the shaman took off his coat, I could see a body of ridges and scars. Then he pulled the knife out again, and I physically jumped back. But he did not move toward me--he plunged it into his thigh. Blood spurted out and landed on me. I was shocked, and a split second later, he was pulling something from the wound. The shaman handed it to me. I was *so* grossed out . . . but I could not refuse something he'd cut from himself--or so it seemed. I took it, feeling stunned. While I was holding it, the monk translator had gone and returned with a bucket of water, which he poured over the gory object. It was a five-inch piece of wood. It was the exact opposite of a river tooth: It had two knurled and yet perfect holes where the knots would have attached to the small trunk--and they were both heart-shaped. I had never seen a piece of driftwood like it in either Fa's or my collections. It was like a missing piece of myself . . . two peas in a pod . . . a perfect natural representation of my missing Fa.

I was staggered, and both Marie-Madeleine and Devi held me up. Devi was about to take her coat off and give it to me. But I pulled my arms back and stepped away from them. I took the shaman's cloak and slowly donned it. It was very heavy; it was still warm, and instead of smelling foul, it had a sweet musk smell. I handed my coat to the shaman. I was the shaman now, and I held his gaze. His face was a maze of wrinkles, but his eyes were the same pure pools of wild calm that I'd seen in Liam's eyes that day on the river. He gave me a big, toothless grin, and I gave him a blast of my pearly whites.

The giant *rag-dung* horns blasted, and Padmasambhava entered the courtyard with an oversized *vajra* thunderbolt. He came looking for the shaman, who stood next to me. The shaman cowered in his white coat, and I moved between Padmasambhava and the shaman and stood my ground. Padmasambhava pointed his giant thunderbolt at me, and I took the ritual bone knife from the cloak and raised it toward Padmasambhava. Everyone stopped moving, and you could hear a collective gasp. I turned it so the hilt pointed toward Padmasambhava and the blade toward my heart. I held it there in the silence. Then Padmasambhava turned his thunderbolt around and did the same. We stood there again for some moments, then Padmasambhava stepped toward me and handed me the thunderbolt and I handed him the ritual knife. We made an exchange. The monks and locals together let out high-pitched, throat-singer-like yells, and everyone began to clap and dance.

Ponies were now being led into the courtyard amidst the festivities. Soon after, one of the locals helped Marie-Madeleine onto one pony. But since the ponies were so short, it was easy just to leap onto their backs-- which Devi and I did.

Because it was led by the Lama, it was a stately procession up the mountain. The path was narrow and fell nearly vertically on one side. The horses were walking slowly but surefootedly on a narrower path than I would have ever been comfortable with. I could not look to my right--it was straight down thousands of feet; more as we continued upward.

The translator was riding on a pony behind me, so I asked him about these Tibetan horses.

"In Tibet and the western part of Nepal, we are horse people. Our main import is tea, and our export has traditionally been horses. The two main breeds are the Riwoche horse and the Nangchen horse. The Nangchen is suited for games, races, and handling livestock; and these

Riwoche horses that we are riding are strong and amazingly surefooted. It has been said that as the Riwoche has been bred in isolation for many thousands of years, it is the link between the wild and domestic horse."

I named my horse "Powa"; I was not sure what it meant in Tibetan, but I liked it that I had Horse Powa. I asked Devi what her horse's name was, and she said Wind . . . Windhorse. My big black cloak tinkled and clanged as we moved up the mountain.

When we got to a high plateau, everyone dismounted and tied their horses to a long wooden post. There was some hay put down for them. At one end of the plateau there was a ridge-like spur that came down from the heights that were obscured by clouds. Below us snaked a glacier down a white valley that in the distance became brown and then green. We were above the tree line and about to head above the dark rocks into a land of pristine white. Porters and young monks carried large baskets of what I did not know.

"How high do you think we are?" I asked Devi.

"Pretty sure we're just shy of 17,000 feet."

"Why are we going still higher?" I asked the translator.

The group started to form a walking procession up the spur.

"We are going up to a lake."

"You mean a frozen lake."

"No, open water."

"That's not possible, everything's frozen up here . . . Ohhh, we must be going up to a hot spring!"

Devi and the translator had a good laugh but would not answer my questions. They just kept saying, "You'll see, you'll see."

Stoking the Fires Within

The path became narrower and narrower. The spur we were on was rising up above the glacier that snaked below us thousands of feet below on either side. You had to carefully place just one foot in front of the other, making sure it was steady before lifting the next. The drums had gone silent; there were only our breaths and each footstep. Complete focus. The light on the horizon took a long time to fade but as it did, the clouds around us cleared, and the full moon rose big and bright from down the valley behind us. Ahead were three soaring white peaks that were tinged to peach by the setting sun. From the flanks of each of those mountains, a glacier curved gracefully into one mighty glacier that we were now climbing above on this spur. It was like we were climbing the back of a dragon's tail. Then, as we came over a rise, I saw it: the impossibility of a blue-green lake surrounded by miles and miles of pure white. There were these little tridents of silver planted in the ground, as this was a pilgrimage site.

I was sure there was some geothermal heat source, so I was ready to take a swim. Fa had taught me to swim in cold water. The secret he told me was that water only goes down to zero degrees--so if it's liquid, and it's minus twenty outside, that water will still only be zero or above. So you can go in and even warm up in the water. Just get out of the cold wind when you come out. It was true; we did breathing exercises, and I learned not to panic when I first went into the cold water and to regulate my breathing till I became relaxed and it went subnormal and became blissful.

Devi and Marie-Madeleine came over. Devi was very hardy from her mountain-climbing and not afraid of the cold. Marie-Madeleine was older but in good shape; however, I was worried about how she'd be able to take the cold.

At the same time, the monks and porters were unloading the baskets and creating a mountain of cloth towels. I joked with Devi and Marie-Madeleine that it was going to be "Yalbang Full Moon Spa Night at 17,000 feet."

They looked at me as though I were slightly crazy.

"Don't worry about me," I said, "I'm used to cold water."

Devi said, "Why don't you take a boot off and dip your toe in."

"No need," I replied.

"I suggest you try," said Marie-Madeleine.

"Okay." I slipped off my boot and sock and put my foot into the water at the edge of the lake.

I immediately yanked it out. "Ow!" I cried. "That's not water, that's fire."

"Yes," said Marie-Madeleine, "it's highly salinized water. No matter how cold it gets, it never freezes."

"Ohhhh," I replied, letting that sink in. This was a whole different league.

"Watch out!" I cried, as I saw the monks soaking the towels.

More laughs from Devi and Marie-Madeleine. They soak and freeze the towels and then use their body heat to melt the frozen towels. The monk who melts the most towels wins.

My mouth dropped open, I had no words. This was crazy.

"There's no way you can melt frozen towels with your almost naked body at this altitude."

"Seeing is believing," said Devi.

"We're a team," said Marie-Madeleine. "I have been told some secrets of generating heat by *tum-mo* by Alexandra, who was a master."

"Great," said Devi, "we will certainly need them. But I think I know a trick that can give us a head start. It will take all the monks by surprise and create a psychological advantage."

"As long as it doesn't involve going into the lake," I suggested.

"It does--but hear me out. We run in yelling and screaming."

"That would be impossible *not* to do, like not yelling out while being burnt at the stake," I suggested.

"We run in, submerge ourselves, and then come up slowly, giving our breathing and heart rate time to slow down. That will give us a big psychological advantage, then the blood will rush to the surface to heat us up; it's called paradoxical stripping. As this heat comes to the surface, we will feel remarkably warm and we can melt some towels."

"That sounds great, but how do we get in the water in the first place? It's way below zero."

"I think I can help with that," said Marie-Madeleine. "Ray, you named your horse 'Powa.' I belong to an organization based in Africa called POWA, People Opposing Women Abuse. There is so much violence against women on this planet. Dedicate this sacrifice--that will not harm you--to the millions of women who are right now suffering abuse. Let's dedicate these few moments of pain and discomfort to them and the wish that we live in a world free of violence."

"I can do that," I said. "I can go into that lake and climb that mountain if I believe it would make a difference."

Devi said, "Any sacrifice does make a difference as it strengthens our hearts and our wills to become the difference."

We took off our coats, held our hands together high in the air, and, yelling POOOOWWWAAA! we ran into the lake of cold fire. I let go of Devi's hand and dove. The torchlight illuminated the strange depths that went down and down into endless darkness. My body was on fire, even my eyeballs, but still I squinted into the darkness and I saw someone swimming below me. That was impossible, but then I felt like a blanket that was heated over a wood stove was being wrapped around my heart. It was as real and as strong a feeling of love as I'd ever felt in Fa's presence. I kept my mind clear and left behind my body to go through the pain of the intense cold. I could not come up--I did not want to leave that love that I had so pined for--for nine long years.

Then I saw Devi swimming down toward me. Her long, flowing hair and her strong body seemed so out of place, here. She grabbed my arm and started pulling me up. We both burst through the surface together and after a few gasping breaths, I was calm and smiling, and she was looking at me worried.

Marie-Madeleine was waiting on the shore and handed us dry towels.

The monks and lay people were looking at us in amazement. Then a single voice started chanting "Powa, Powa," and others took up the chant. Devi was right--our blood was being rerouted to the surface as part of an emergency survival mechanism.

The translator came over when we were drying ourselves and told us we were amazing. That helped my skin glow a bit more. He said few people were able to enter the water, mostly wandering *sadhus* and *tantrikas*. But as a sacred lake, complete immersion in it meant we had erased the mistakes of a lifetime. Wow, that felt pretty good. Starting with a clean slate!

I thanked him, and the three of us women went over to where the frozen towels were lined up, and we sat on towels next to each other. Twenty or so monks stripped to their *lungis*, or boxers, and took up their positions on the frozen towels. The competition had begun!

It was definitely numbing. Yet I could see its value in controlling the monks' libidos. After a few minutes, the effect of our blood rushing to the surface was diminishing.

"Okay," said Marie-Madeleine, "here's the technique that Alexandra taught me.

"First, visualize yourself as hollow, like a balloon. Your skin is glowing, and on the inside there is only empty space. Take a few moments to strongly establish this visualization.

"Next, visualize three channels with a '*central channel*' about one centimetre in diameter from your perineum (the area between the anus and the scrotum in men and between the anus and the vulva in women), to the crown of your head and two '*side channels*' going in through the nostrils up to the third eye and then going down either side of the central channel, merging at just below the navel. All the 'channels' are hollow. Take a moment to establish this visualization.

"Now the next step is the most important in generating the heat: Imagine your breath energy going down the two side channels and merging into the central channel just below the navel (a few centimetres in front of the spine). Imagine a very small and very hot ball of light in the central channel and your breath igniting this fiery ball and making it extremely hot. Now hold the breath there in that ball of heat at the navel for five to fifteen seconds (experienced yogis can hold the breath here for several minutes). If you get dizzy or lightheaded, pause until it passes.

"Finally, as you are holding the ball of heat inside the central channel, draw energy up from below and down from above and trap the ball of heat. Draw it up by activating the perineum muscle (like you are holding back from urinating), hold this muscle and lock it in. Simultaneously swallow some saliva down to get the feeling of pushing down on the ball of heat at the navel and lock it in.

"Do what feels best for you to get the sense you are locking in a tremendous amount of energy in a tiny space at the navel.

"Now release all the energy you have created--straight up through the central channel and bursting out the top of your head like a fountain. As the energy rushes up through the central channel, it blows away any blockages in all the chakras from the solar plexus, the heart, the throat, the third eye, and crown chakra. Mastering this is the first stage of *tum-mo*."

"The first stage?"

"Yes--monks practise this for years."

Monks were now beginning to remove melted towels from under their bodies and new, frozen ones were placed under them. We did the same, all the time practising the *tum-mo* steps that Marie-Madeleine had taught us. I got the sense that it really did work.

How visualizations can control bodily functions is truly amazing.

Devi said, "Scientists have come to this country and measured the heat produced by *tum-mo* and confirmed that there is a significant physiological effect created by these visualizations."

Older monks and lay people were soaking and freezing great piles of towels, while the pile of towels beside each meditator were growing higher. We started to look over and I could see that there were monks who whose piles were two or three towels higher than ours.

"We're losing the lead!" Devi exclaimed. "We need to produce more heat."

"I have an idea. Love has energy as well, and I bet it can produce heat. While we're visualizing the channels and the ball of fire, let's add another layer. Let's imagine the ball is love; and while we are working with that ball of love, moving and trapping it, let's put a loved one in our mind's eye. When we release that ball of love up through the top of our heads, let that love blast the person we are holding in our mind's eye. That might enhance the effect and block the heat a second time."

Marie-Madeleine said, "It's worth a try."

So we gave it a try. It took a while to add another layer to the visualization, but I saw how you could add layer upon layer to these visualizations. This was just a teaser exercise compared to the immense visualizations that adepts and lamas could do.

It was working! We were pulling into the lead. We'd melted four towels in the time that most others had melted two. As I'm describing it, it sounds like a race; but it must be one of the slowest competitions on earth, and most of what's happening is being visualized on the inside. So it looks like almost nothing is happening in this remote little spot on the roof of the world. A nearly bare person stands up, one towel is removed and examined by a kind of judge and then added to the pile beside each person and a new frozen towel replaces it. It's all very slow and melodramatic. Yet amazingly big things are being explored and undertaken on inner realms.

Monks are starting to drop out of the competition, and Marie-Madeleine says, "That's my Everest. I hand over the torch, so to speak, to you and Devi."

"You are amazing!" we both piped in.

Marie-Madeleine stood up, made sure she was dry, put her big yak coat on, and continued to sit with us. We could hear the boom of avalanches roaring down the slopes around us punctuating the deep, absolute silence. As the hours passed, we visualized on. I sent so much love energy to Grandsy, Fa, and Mum that I even had some to spare for Rai the Honey Hunter.

Finally I felt that was it for me. I said to Devi, "You're going to have to carry the torch for me as well."

As Devi opened her eyes, a lazy, blissful smile crossed her face, and she whispered, "Will do."

It was now down to Devi and four monks. Time seemed to stand still. I was grateful for that great black Shaman's cloak; it seemed to have its own heat source.

Finally, only Devi and one monk remained. The piles of towels beside them had now refrozen and formed a solid tower twice their height.

Just as the first light of dawn broke from behind the mountains, the final monk called for his fellow adepts to lift him off the towel. Everyone was absolutely quiet and we saw a perfect ray of light burst between the two sacred mountains directly above us and bathe the lake in light.

Marie-Madeleine and I came over to lift Devi from the last thawed towel, and she folded her hands over her heart and slowly rose up from her cross-legged posture.

Devi was smiling, I was crying, and Marie-Madeleine was ecstatic.

"I need to get the blood flowing," said Devi. "What say we test how sure-footed these ponies are?"

"What about your cloak?" asked Marie-Madeleine.

"I want to feel the wind against my skin. I want to feel everything. I just need to get my blood really flowing."

We were ready to agree to anything Devi wanted at this moment.

"Get your ponies, girls, and let's ride!" said Devi.

The three of us leapt onto our Riwoche horses, yelled HA! and rode flat-out across the high plateau.

Devi yelled, "POWA, POWA!" and all together we yelled, "POWA,

POWA, POWA!"

At that moment we were three powerful women, and I include myself, one Black Rider, one White Rider, and a Tan rider with flecks of white, surrounded by peaks lit up like flaming matchsticks. Streaks of golden light flew through the plateau and ignited the crystals of ice in the air around us.

Perhaps we are the New Apocalypse, recognizing and transforming the demons within, so others can live in a world where there are no massacres, no apocalyptic levels of emotional immaturity.

There was little time for reflection; moments later, we were at the end of the plateau and charging down the narrow switchback path that we had so carefully navigated on the way up. The ponies seemed to be drawing strength from the faith we had in them as they flew down the mountain, not putting one hoof an inch out of place. If Shambhala was anywhere it was here, right in this moment. Minutes later, we had covered the ground that took over an hour on the way up and we were once again in the courtyard of Yalbang Monastery.

We wasted no time in stoking the fire in the hermitage and heating lots of tea. In the corner of the hermitage was an old four-legged bath that someone must have carried all the way up from Kathmandu. We used every pot to heat water up for the bath. With Devi in first, we started with cool water and, after a few minutes, we added warmer and warmer water to slowly raise her core temperature. Once Devi was warm, we each took turns until we all ended up in the big bathtub drinking tea laced with *raksi*, creating quite a ruckus. Party night in Yalbang!

Naga Teeth

Next morning, we slept right through the morning *rag-dung* wake-up call and meditation. We slept until we heard the bell signalling the mid-morning teaching. Groggily we each opened one eye, and Marie-Madeleine led the way in getting up, stoking the fire, making some more tea. Devi pulled herself out of bed and poured a bit of *raksi* in the tea and stated, "Hair of the dog." None of us argued, although to me it did seem a bit sacrilegious to drink before a teaching. Then I thought back to last night: if the sins of a lifetime had been erased, then time to start collecting them again.

We knocked back the tea and had a little *tsampa*. Devi then mixed the tea into the *tsampa* and rolled it into little balls in her palms and handed us a couple.

"This should improve the teachings," she said.

We raced out the door, me still in my black cloak, and into the courtyard. There were smiles and nods from all the students as we sat down among them. The Lama entered the courtyard. I remembered to draw in my legs. Things started in the usual way with the chanting and the prayer wheel and the *vajra*.

"The mind is a stream . . . your mind is a stream, my mind is a stream, together our minds are a river. Look at how it flows; become a river watcher, a river keeper. Keep it pure, keep it vibrant. Make sure there are pools of still water and big rapids of intention and effort. But don't let it get stagnant. Also protect your mindstream from the mindstream of others--especially turbulent mindstreams. Watch and see how others affect your mindstream. Is there someone who is frequently disturbing yours? They are a teacher for you, learn how to protect yourself and not let that happen. This is very important--especially as we are living in community.

"How do you observe that stream? Throw a stick into the stream--does it get stuck? Does it get swept away? Watch its movements."

A stick into a stream--that was sounding like a river tooth, I thought.

"Now," continued the Lama, "see the tiny self, what you perceive as you--your consciousness in this vast time-stream floating through many lifetimes. We begin as a freshly fallen tree, and through many lifetimes we are worn down to our true and essential self. That essence is indestructible."

I was blown away. The Lama was speaking of the journey of the river tooth through many lifetimes.

"These resonated knots that are our essential selves, we call river teeth!" I literally cried out.

"Ha, ha, again we are on the same wavelength. These what you call river teeth, we call *naga teeth*; teeth of the river spirits."

"You have them here, too?" Then I realized how stupid this was.

"Of course. Each 'tooth' is unique but also there are aspects that are universal, invariant."

I popped a couple of *tsampa* balls.

"This flux, this river, these *naga teeth* are worn down through the forces of lifetimes. Go to the river, each of you; find some *naga teeth*. When you begin this search, it might take you some time to recognize your first tooth. Or, perhaps you have one already but do not know it? Keep searching, keep collecting and noticing what is unique and what is invariant. One day you will be meditating in a shallow river, and light will leap up from the stones, and you will see every piece of wood in the river on its way to becoming a perfect *naga tooth* . . . a Buddha, a bodhisattva."

I started this journey going to the river; met River, who gave me a key that Fa had left me. In that storage unit there was a river tooth, and now this elderly Vajrayana teacher was telling me how we all were river teeth on journeys of transformation through many lifetimes. I could really visualize this. I reached into my hidden pocket where I kept Fa's special river tooth and checked that it was there. I stood up and walked up to Lama Riksal.

"I would like to show you the river tooth my father left for me."

The Lama beamed at me and motioned for me to sit down beside him. He chanted and brought out his ritual knife, a *phurba*, his bell, and his *vajra* and he handled them in a very dexterous way that was called a hand mudra. During the last of the mudras, the bell rang out simply and clearly. He explained that now I was free of all hindrances in my mind and heart.

I reached into my secret pocket and pulled out Fa's first river tooth and carefully handed it to Lama Riksal. He took it in his hands and turned it over a few times, looking closely at it. Then he enclosed it in his hands and chanted. Finally, he held it up between his fingers so others could see it.

"This," he said, "is a perfect river tooth. You may never see one like it in many lifetimes of searching."

Everyone strained their necks to get a good look at it.

"Close your eyes, Ray; what do you see?"

"I see that Grandsy is the perfect river tooth and I have the Pearl of Great Price in my heart and that is the medicine to bring her back to life."

"Then what are you doing here sitting beside an old man? Your Grandsy is a Bodhisattva. Make haste! I give you the horse you named POWA, who will surefootedly take you where you wish to go."

With a flourish of his hands he waved me away. I walked away with tears of joy streaming down my face. I walked through a sea of smiling faces nodding and saying "Namaste . . . Namaste . . . Namaste." Devi and Marie-Madeleine followed me from the courtyard.

I knew it was time for me to leave. I had to meet Mum and Liam on the Karnali River. I checked the dates, and it was too late to meet them at Simikot. The only way was to intercept them on the river.

Devi asked, "Would you be willing to join Marie-Madeleine and me on our Quest to Mt. Kailash and what we believe to be the true door to Shambhala? Afterwards, we can accompany you back to the Karnali River or Kathmandu if you wish.

"Ray," Marie-Madeleine, said, "you must truly listen to your intuition and follow your heart."

"I do so want to join you both and continue the Quest to Shambhala, but I am ready and want to return to Mt. Albert and to Grandsy. I now know that if she and I work together, she will come back to life, and I will gain the lessons of a lifetime. But to do that, I must finish this journey--meet Mum and Liam and tie up one little loose end."

"And would that loose end be a boy?" laughed Devi.

"It might be," I said shyly.

"And a Honey Hunter with the same namesake?"

"Getting very warm."

"Hot, I'd say. But don't forget there's a false entrance to Shambhala and the Land of the Immortals in the vicinity. I know it has something to do with the Honey Hunters, but it was as though once I stopped believing in it, it eluded me."

"Who is going to guide you to the river, Ray?" asked Marie-Madeleine.

"The monk translator told me he knows the route through a cave that descends to the Karnali River. From there, I hope to intercept Mum and Liam."

Technically, I hadn't lied--although it was the translator who spoke the Bon shaman's words. But I knew they might not continue on their quest if they knew that I was travelling with the shaman.

Devi said, "Be very careful. Remember, the nuns called the Palace of the Three Veils the entrance to Shambhala, and now I believe that it leads to a false paradise. I guess after all they are sworn protectors, so I should have expected that they would try to trick us."

Up to this point, Marie-Madeleine had been very quiet. "Ray, I have stopped at the Karnali on the way here and placed the ashes of Alexandra and her son Yongden into the river so now they flow from the Sacred Mountain to all the world. So my journey to this river is complete. But I owe it to you to tell you what I know about Shambhala from Alexandra so you do not wander into a false Shambhala. There are many false Shambhalas--the West is full of them.

"Alexandra did mention the Karnali but also the source of three other rivers: the Indus, Tsangpo, and Brahmaputra. Often she made a reference to a 'door in the sky,' and in her last words it was evident she was searching for this in her mind's eye. There is also a circumambulation, or, as the Tibetans call, it a Kora nearby. These clues we must interpret."

In no time, Devi and Marie-Madeleine were packed. The Lamas are not into big farewells, and so soon they were ready to leave--fortunately before the Bon shaman arrived. We made small exchanges of precious things with each other. Adventures bring people so close together that it was difficult for us to part. We hugged and held each other. We also really praised each other for the qualities that we saw and expressed how we believed in each other's quest. We didn't rush this; we went lovingly into details. At the end of an hour, each of us surely felt beautifully seen, appreciated for the best in ourselves, and connected for life.

I watched and waved to my dear friends Devi and Marie-Madeleine till they were out of sight. They were on their way to Mount Kailash. It was difficult to not go with them; but the Bon-Po shaman had said that he had seen Fa go through a door in the sky. So perhaps I was not finished with that door, and Devi and Marie-Madeleine were of course looking for clues for me. But Fa had clearly said, "Look after Grandsy, she is the heart of the world." So I knew in my heart this was the right choice.

CHAPTER FIVE
REALM OF ILLUSIONS

Doors in the Sky

A lonely hermitage on a mountain peak,
Towering above a thousand others
One-half is occupied by an old monk,
The other by a cloud!
Last night it was stormy
And the cloud was blown away;
After all a cloud is not equal
To the old man's quiet way.
Ryokwan

When the Bon-Po shaman arrived, he did nothing to allay hesitation at following him. My white yak coat was streaked with red that was presumably blood. He somehow had got his ceremonial tools back that were, last time I noticed, attached to my coat. He gave me a big, toothless grin when I looked at them surprised.

"Do no good for you," he stated.

"You can speak English?"

"Little."

"You said you could take me to a cave that leads to the Karnali?"

"Yes, right on the Karnali, at a very remote part of the river."

"Where the river comes through a very narrow fissure?"

"Fissure?"

"Narrow crack."

"Yes, that's the exact place."

"That's called God's House!" I burst out.

113

"Yes, it is God's House for sure; we call it the Land of Dewa Chen."

"You can take me to Dewa Chen?"

"Yes, ma'am, if you are sure."

Today the shaman did not seem quite so fierce and somehow more accommodating--and he spoke a surprising amount of English. Liam and Mum would get quite a surprise to see me at the water's edge along the most inaccessible stretch of the Karnali River.

I packed my things into the saddlebags on my new horse friend POWA, said goodbye to Chokyi in the kitchen, and rode down the trail from Yalbang with the Bon shaman, who himself was riding a very fine horse.

"What kind of horse are you riding?"

"A Nangchen horse. It has been kept as a pure breed for many centuries. It only became known to the West in 1994. It has lungs for the high altitude and is fast and agile. It's a Tibetan racehorse."

The shaman took off to demonstrate the speed of his horse. My little pony, Powa, had no inclination to show off, and so we just steadily trotted along. I had mixed feelings about this particular shaman, yet he was willing to take me where I was willing to go. Was this being trusting or simply naive?

The landscape was changing by the hour, from the lush, high-altitude meadows to an arid desert that looked like the Grand Canyon, but BIGGER. I had done some reading on this, and it was one thing to read from a dry Wikipedia page and quite another to experience it with all the senses--so vividly.

Nepal is only 800 kilometres long, with the Himalayas stretching its entire length along its northern border with Tibet. Along its southern border lies India and lush rainforest about 150 meters above sea level. Yet it's a skinny country, only 150 to 250 kilometres wide. This is what makes Nepal a country of such incredible diversity. Three major river systems run through Nepal: the Karnali, the Sun Kosi, and the Kali Gandiki. These run from the high Tibetan plateau across Nepal, right through the Himalaya into the Indian subcontinent. A full 50 per cent of all river water that enters India comes through these three great river systems. That is a huge volume, and these river systems have carved mammoth pathways for millions of years and are the main way of crossing the Himalayas without climbing over the mountains themselves.

The greatest trade route the world has ever known, the Silk Road, has used these routes to exchange the wealth of China with the wealth of India and the rest of the world.

Even though it appeared empty now, when empires were rising and falling, vast quantities of goods were moving through these very corridors.

The reason it was becoming so dry and desertified was that as we crossed the height of land, all the wet climate of the Indian subcontinent fell along the southern length of Nepal in the rainforest. The entire northern border was in what's called a rain-shadow. The southern border gets as much as 550 centimetres (216 inches) of rain, and the northern border zone that we were entering gets as little as 16 centimetres (6.3 inches).

The valley around the river was lush and green, with neat little postage stamp-sized fields; but above, the mountains rose from an earthy ochre to the brilliant purity of the sunlit heights. Great cloud shadows moved across this vast theatre animated by expert stagehands. About 250 million years ago, where I was standing was the great sea of Tethys between the continents of Gondwana and Pangaea. Then, about 50 million years ago, the Indian and the Eurasian Tectonic Plates collided and formed the Himalayas. There are fossilized seashells on the summit of Mt. Everest.

I was infinitesimal in the immensity and also strangely becoming more in the greatness of the whole. This in itself was a spiritual experience.

"Look there!" I shouted. "Those are Doors in the Sky!"

"Yes, they are like the caves that I was speaking of. Entire villages and spiritual communities have lived in caves like those going back maybe 18,000 years."

"How do you know this?"

"Part of the way I know is from the ancestral stories of the Bon; long before Buddhism arrived, we passed our history down in the oral tradition. I was the translator on a number of National Geographic expeditions to this region. That's how I improved my English. I don't use it much, though, as a shaman. The local people believe that once their history is spoken in English, it is lost. However, my experience of the National Geographic was that although they were exploiting our stories for their own purposes, they were also interested in preserving our history and keeping the artifacts here. But there has been so much looting over the years that suspicion runs deep."

"You said you saw Fa go through a door into the sky."

"Yes, but in Nepal we have literally thousands of doors in the sky."

"Oh, so now you tell me."

"I only told you what I saw. It's for you to interpret."

"How do people get into those cave entrances that are hundreds and sometimes thousands of feet vertically up a cliff face with no stairs? They look totally inaccessible."

"Ha, ha . . . if you ask the local people, they will say the lamas can fly."

"Do you know?"

"Yes; why should I tell you?"

"Because I'll give you your cloak back if you do."

"I don't want my cloak back; I like yours."

"Please, tell me anyway."

"We know that the exposed caves are visible because over the past thousands of years, the sandstone cliffs calved off, like icebergs, and that left some of the internal rooms exposed."

"Really!"

"Really."

"How fantastic. I was seeing twenty caves in a row and also caves on multiple levels. There must have been entire villages living in those caves."

"Yup--kept us safe from those armies marching along the Silk Road and made the traders and their wealth pretty easy prey for us. Ha, till the cliffs calved and we're standing there in our *lungis*.

"But what they don't know . . ."

"Yes?"

"What they don't know is that there are many, many more caves where the cliffs did not calve off. You don't think any locals will be showing them where those cave systems are."

"Why can't Western explorers and archaeologists find them?"

"Because they can't go around rolling back every rock they see in our country. There are many, many cave villages and mortuaries that even we've forgotten the whereabouts of.

"Mortuaries or charnel grounds, as we call them. We had entire villages for the dead, like a cemetery, but with rooms, each containing their sacred tools and whatever they need for their next life."

"I can't believe it . . . you're telling stories."

It was an old trick that Fa used on me, accusing me of telling stories to get more information. I was just so curious and I felt like these "Doors in the Sky" contained the best clue I had to Fa's whereabouts.

"Ha, Ray, I can see the little game you're playing, and if you play with masters of the game, you will lose every time; but perhaps you will grow a little wiser. So I am going to tell you something else."

"Yes!" I responded enthusiastically.

"There is a very big village not far from here."

"Where?" All I could see were a few huts along the river.

"It's on the other side of the bend in the river; you can't see it yet."

So we travelled on in silence, but within me there was a growing excitement. Was the shaman going to show me something that had been kept a secret from outsiders? I knew this was a land of hidden teachings and places. Fa told me they are called *beyuls*. He was always off looking for *beyuls* around the world. When we went to walk in nature and we arrived at a spot that had a special feeling and beauty to it, he'd tell me it was a *beyul*. So I was taught from a young age to seek *beyuls*, hidden places that only those with certain levels of consciousness can see.

To make conversation, I asked, "Are there any other reasons besides looting that your people chose to live underground in caves?"

"Of course. With so many traders came not only goods but also ideas from many cultures. We found that we had to believe ourselves to be special, for our gods to be special, our story special, for us to have the ability to make progress as a people. We lived along the Silk Road, now you live along the Internet. Same thing. We learned to enjoy what the traders brought in terms of goods but to also maintain our own culture so we could fulfill our destiny."

"But you borrowed ideas from Buddhism and, with only metaphysical battles between Buddhists and Bon Pos, you integrated."

"Yes--we didn't close ourselves off from the world, we adapted and evolved our culture through an evolution of the stories we told. But we changed only as fast as our stories could keep pace with our culture. Any faster and we'd have disintegrated."

I was fascinated, but we'd just rounded the bend, and there was no village; instead, there was something geographically very unusual. The river, the entire Karnali, one of the highest-volume rivers on earth, disappeared. The valley just ended in a cliff. As we drew closer, I could see that the river disappeared into a giant cave at the base of the cliff. This was the inaccessible section of the river that I'd heard about. The section Liam was trying to enter and kayak.

"That's where God's House is!" I pointed and shouted.

"Ha, a little knowledge can be dangerous. It is indeed God's House."

"Can you take me there?"

"Do you know what you are asking?"

"Yes, of course."

"We must ask the Gurung villagers. They are honey hunters, and these cliffs are filled with beehives that they have lived off of for many thousands of years. They must agree to take you."

I was going to tell him that my first big Quest when I was eleven was to the Kalahari to warn the Queen of the Queen Bees in Africa that big agribusiness wanted to genetically modify bees to pollinate only their company's crops. But right now I was more interested in these bees.

The Bon shaman said, "These bees are twice the size of European and African varieties of bees."

Of course--they're Himalayan, they'd have to be twice as big, I thought.

"The honey is also very special, like nowhere else in the world. You must be--"

"All honey is special, no matter where it's found," I replied.

"Ahh, little big girl who think she knows it all. Ha, you will see."

We started to make our way back to the Gurung village. It was a well-ordered little village, but perhaps the people there were a little more reserved than I expected. The shaman told me that I'd have to be prepared for some long negotiations. I leaned my backpack against a tree and sat down. We were offered tea. Some way into the discussion, a Maoist rebel joined in to make sure that a fair deal was struck.

The shaman said, "The Gurungs want to be sure that I understand that people do not return from God's House. That it's a one-way trip; they would take me up to the top of the cliff and remove the entrance stone and I would have to make my way from there."

An entranceway to the river through the cliff . . . that was so cool and a bit creepy.

"Thank the Gurungs for me. Tell them that I am meeting family and friends on the other side."

They nodded their heads quite seriously.

"The Gurungs want to know what you are going to do with your horse."

"Tell them they can keep Powa, as long as they call him by name and take care of him till I send someone to get him. He can do any task, just not pull a plough."

"They say that's acceptable to them."

"They will lead you up the cliff tonight. They say day is too hot, night is safer."

"Okay, tell them I'm well-rested."

"This is where we part, Ray. But to keep you safe, I'm going to give you my *phurba*, my ceremonial knife. It will help you slay obstructions in your path and also transform negative energies such as the 'three poisons,' which are attachment, ignorance, and aversion."

I turned it over in my hand. I had admired it when the shaman gave me his coat. It was three-sided and more like a ceremonial tent peg than a knife. It had the head of Ganesh as a handle.

I wished him well, but to be honest I was relieved to see him go and thankful that things had gone as well as they did.

Since I arrived, I had been secretly hoping that this would be Rai's village, but I didn't see him and was too shy to ask. When they had gathered torches and a few supplies, four Gurungs and myself headed toward the cliff face. As we got closer, I got a sense of the immensity of the scale. Everything, including the bees, was at least twice the scale of the Rocky Mountains. There were bones and a lot of debris along the base of the cliff. One of the younger men managed to communicate that the cliffs are more likely to crumble during the day, and it's a dangerous path. Then, only when we were right at the base could I see that carved into the cliff were steps only about a foot wide. They were the same ochre colour and so could not be seen except close up. We began to move up them single file. As the cliff was cut out to a height of only five feet, you literally had to crouch as you climbed. It was a night I'd never forget.

God's House

One side was hollowed into the cliff; on the other, you were climbing to the heavens. The Gurungs had put the torches out to conserve them, and it was only just possible to make out the steps. The cliff to my left was now black, but to my right the dark night was riven by the Milky Way. We were plodding toward the stars . . . we were stardust returning. I couldn't let my thoughts wander too far, as there were only twelve inches of step and no railing.

Time literally stood still. Then, ahead, the Gurangs stopped at a place where there was an opening into the cliff face. This was my first cave in the region. They welcomed me in. The room was much larger than I expected, and it had beautiful, soft, rounded shapes. Nothing was square. The room was lit with hundreds of butter candles. They told me an old monk was very sick and had been dying for six months. "Very bad diarrhoea."

A friend had talked me into taking one full course of Cipro with me in case of serious bacterial infection. I did not want to give it up--it was like a safety net. But as I went over to where a bed was cut out of the cave, I saw the tiniest shape of a body under the blankets. It could have been Fa at the end of the road in some faraway place. The moment the old monk saw me, a big smile broke from his cracked lips. I knew that I could give up my safety net. I took the Cipro out of my backpack and marked a calendar out in the sandy floor of the cave, indicating to the nun who was taking care of him when to give him the pills for a full dose. She understood and thanked me. It was still a long way up, so we left the cave and continued like ants up the cliff face.

Then, just when I'd given up hope of ever reaching the top, there we were, high above the river on the plateau. We walked along a scrubby path beside the cliff face for some time till we came to a little depression with a large boulder at one end of it. All four of them using some large poles pried back the boulder, revealing an entrance. A real secret tunnel! One of the men reached into his bag and pulled out a live cock and, handing it to me, said it would be needed for an offering.

I had no idea there would be people in this tunnel.

I checked with them, "Are you sure this leads to God's House?"

"Oh, yes," they nodded. "God's House."

They handed me a torch and whistled loudly down the tunnel. Just as my eyes adjusted to the light, I looked around, and the large boulder was being rolled back into place. Now there was no way but forward.

My torch lit up the circular stairs carved into the sedimentary rock. All along the stairwell there were symbols and even elaborate colourful murals of what looked like the lives of enlightened Lamas. Some I could recognize as clearly Buddhist, but others looked wilder. Every so often, I came to a landing where there was a single heavy wooden door. I was curious to see what was behind it, but each of them were secured by an ancient lock. However, I knew I needed to go way, way down to reach the level of the river. I did keep count: When I got to the thirteenth level, I came out into an open area where there were no obvious stairs continuing down. In the centre of the landing was simply a table carved out of the sandstone, and on it was a silver bell. I rang the bell, and out from behind a wall came an attractive, well-dressed Tibetan woman with a towel and slippers.

She said, "English, yes."

"Canadian," I replied.

"English?" She said with more hesitation.

"English," I replied.

"Ah, welcome to Spa."

"SPA!" I could not contain my disbelief but also was this not my greatest wish? Travelling through this Kingdom of Lo, one dusty arid plain after another . . . all those stairs up the cliffside . . . and now I come to a spa! I would have been a bit more encouraged to see Scandinavians running it, but let's not quibble. The towels looked clean and the slippers inviting.

The Spa at the End of the World

I introduced myself and found out the woman's name was Tashi.

I gave Tashi the cock, and she thanked me (*Thu-chi che*), then led me into the change rooms, which were simple but well thought-out.

I asked Tashi, "Who designed this?"

"Romans came through here long ago."

I had many more questions but it seemed we'd nearly reached the limits of Tashi's English.

Fortunately, I had my bathing suit in my backpack.

Again, the door closed behind me as I was changing, so there was no way but forward. I took my small bag of sacred possessions and passport with me as I walked through the winding passage that led from the change room. The air was getting heavier and increasingly moist. It was not going to be *tum-mo* this time. As the passage opened up, it was hard to make anything out, as the air was so foggy. What I could make out was a great pool in the centre of a very large cave. From this pool there was steam rising up in great swirls off the water. There were definitely people in the pool. I noticed that generally at one end the fog was denser. Although it appeared to be one great room, there were openings leading off it, and it looked like you could swim into the other rooms. There were all sorts of sculptures and tiled mosaics adorning the place. Just no tapestries--I guess because of the moisture.

Just then it dawned on me that the shaman must have meant this was "God's House," rather than the rapids with the same name. Perhaps someone named the rapids after this place? Oh, yes, *the big little know-it-all. Ha, you will get a surprise.* Now the shaman's words were coming back to me and making sense.

As I walked around, I could vaguely make out a wide variety of nationalities. I decided to take the plunge and slip into the pool near an older gentleman with white hair tied in a ponytail. The water was hot but mineral-rich and relaxing. There were spots carved out that just fit your body, and you could lean your head against the sandstone. I had not admitted how exhausted I was; this was too good to be true.

After a few minutes, the older man said, "I'm Heinz. Welcome to the Spa at the End of the World."

"You can speak English," I said surprised.

"Yes, and seven other languages. I'm afraid that sounded like a brag. I didn't mean it to be. Perhaps there is, after all, some ego left in this old man," Heinz said with a laugh.

"I have more questions, and they are not about whether you have any ego or not," I stated perhaps overly forcefully. "How did you come to be here?"

"I'm a geologist, and this is an obvious place to come and study. The formations tell us in such visible language the story of the earth. More specifically, my interest is in a formation called the Tethyan Sequence."

"You mean the Sea of Tethys."

"Yes, exactly. These rocks all around us formed in the Sea of Tethys at a depth of several kilometres."

"That is very cool." This obviously encouraged him.

"The very soft stone that surrounds us in this room is full of ocean fossils that formed between India and Asia. This mantle extends from the riverbed up to the tops of the world's highest mountains--some eleven kilometres thick. Being formed under the ocean means that the strata are made up of weakly consolidated layers which create ideal conditions for natural cave formation and cave building."

"So everyone comes to Nepal for the mountains, but the real story is taking place under their feet."

"That's it--you've got it. Welcome to the Kingdom of Lo."

"*Beyuls*, as my Fa would call them: places of inner significance."

"Welcome to *Beyul* Central, then."

"So you're in this spa studying geology?" I asked with some suspicion.

"At first, I did think this place could help my work.

"But be careful; do not be lulled into a false sense of security. The Tibetans are not prudes, and this place exists for all stages of the journey."

"The journey to where?"

I have to go. All of a sudden, out of the mist there appeared what looked like a large cat at Heinz's side; then I recognized a shaman of some kind clothed in leopard skins.

Heinz said, "To you this looks like an old medicine woman in skins, but I see what she really is."

"What do you see?" I asked nervously.

"I see things in their true form. Now, I'm going to tell you something important to remember. When the Bear comes, make your way back to the spa. This is now what we call the end of the *Golden Hour*."

I watched Heinz walk away alongside the very feline shaman. There was something strange about this place.

I was still soaking up the heat when a very good-looking man appeared from the misty water and sat near me. I was glad, as I still had lots of questions.

"Where are you from?" he asked.

Even though we were worlds away, it sounded like a pickup line from the local bar in Mt. Albert.

"You first," I said.

"I'm from Persia."

"I thought it was now called Iran."

"My Greek ancestors fought in the Greco-Persian wars during the fifth century BC and never returned to Greece. So we call ourselves Persian."

"Wasn't Persia part of the Ottoman Empire at that time?

He laughed and said, "By the way, my name's Hamid."

"My name's Ray."

"How'd you find out about this place?" That sounded like another Mt.

Albert pickup line. "My grandfather would tell stories about his travels as a trader. He never did find this place but he'd heard about it on his travels. So when I was twenty-five, I set out to find it."

"How long did it take you?"

"Five years, more or less."

"That's a long spiritual quest."

"This is not a spiritual quest for me."

Before I could articulate my surprise, a shaman appeared beside Hamid wearing a bearskin. It was "God's House," after all; I should expect to see shamans.

The Golden Hour

The bear-like shaman handed Hamid a tray with what was clearly honey. Hot tub room service by shamans dressed as bears. I think I could market this. Tibetan salt cave . . . honey bars . . . it could be a whole new thing. Maybe the bears could be the logo. The honeycomb was a beautiful golden red; it was true I hadn't seen anything like it.

The shaman bear turned and pushed the tray of honeycomb toward me. I had no idea if he'd understand me, but I asked, "Could I start with some Tibetan *mo mos* and then have some honey afterwards?"

All I got was a loud, disturbing, "ROAR!"

That's when Hamid told me that they eat only honey in this place.

"Only honey?" I said. I thought I'd never say that. I always considered honey to be the perfect food.

"It's very special Himalayan honey. Known in exclusive circles around the world as 'Mad Honey.'" said Hamid.

"Okay, I might as well try some."

"Not too much to start with," cautioned Hamid.

I'd drunk nearly a cup of honey once at the Big Carrot and eaten the better part of a spear of honey while in the Kalahari. So I picked up a bigger comb than Hamid was pointing to.

"Suit yourself," Hamid said.

The shaman bear lumbered off.

"If you're not here on a spiritual journey, what kind of journey are you here for?"

"Pleasure."

"Pleasure?"

Hamid winked at me, "Pleasure pure and simple."

"Pleasure is not pure or simple."

I could see more and more people converging in the mist. I didn't like where this was headed.

"Where's the cold plunge?" I asked sarcastically.

Hamid pointed over to the left.

"I think you should try it," I said as I got up. On the way over to the cold plunge pool, emerging and disappearing into the mist, I saw people in the most outrageous postures. I had once found the Kama Sutra in Fa's library, and obviously it had made its way over here, as had Buddhism.

I found the cold plunge pool, and it was a big wake-up call. As the blood rushed to my brain, I nearly blacked out. I came to a few moments later, and things were starting to spin and become distorted. Right then I knew what everyone meant by "special" or "mad" honey. It was hallucinogenic. *Those bees--fancy that!* I thought. What I remember next was a snow leopard--a real snow leopard--ambling its way toward me. It looked long into my eyes. I got to see into its eyes, which were the most beautiful blue green, and yet not a flicker of emotion. Then it reached out with its paw and swatted my hand, which was completely limp. I knew I was a total basket case and could feel a stupid grin coming across my face. Next thing I remember, a Bear appeared--yes, a bear, a real bear this time--and picked me up and carried me on its back. I saw something like a raccoon (that's crazy, as I don't think there are raccoons in Nepal) with keys, and after that I was being carried up the stairs. I think I might have vomited a few times.

I was put down somewhere quite comfortable and a young woman bathed my forehead with a cool cloth. I felt safe and so commenced an inner quest.

I also knew that it had thirteen levels, and these had a similar significance to the number of stages of enlightenment. The entire place was a path to awareness and awakening. It was place where time had no significance . . . or did it? I could test out all my hypotheses; I could live out every choice I could imagine. I could test out every timeline. Wow. I vomited a few more times, but the nausea seemed like a small thing compared to what I was seeing. The Bear brought more honey, and I eagerly took it. I thought if I could travel every timeline, then perhaps I could venture beyond this into previous lifetimes. I found I could go back and forth along timelines from many lifetimes. It was a karmic adventure. There were volumes, books and books of adventures, lifetimes of loving and heartbreak that I discovered. Was it real? Somehow this seemed to have no significance here. It appeared in my mind's eye and was a story, and the story was everything. Did any darkness or demons appear? Yes, but they all seemed to be within, and I had a way to either skirt or ignore them.

Next time the Bear appeared, I looked forward to renewing the adventure, and this time I wanted to see if I could travel the timelines of others. YES, it was working. I could look into what appeared to be video footage of the lives of those I knew. It was a kind of *emotional* video. I could feel their emotions as I scrolled through the footage. Actually, this was the first time I became aware that I was not entirely in control of the process. It was as though the playback mechanism was stuck, and I could not pause or stop it. It was fun and a bit shocking to look into Mum's past. She was not always just like she was now or portrayed herself to be. Humph. I hope to remember some of this stuff; it could prove very useful.

I became curious about Liam, so I had a look at his timeline. Wow, a bad boy in his teens. Could I back up and see his childhood? I could, then the rewind seemed to get stuck in reverse and I went right through into his previous lifetime. OH, that *was* bad--he did some bad things and racked up some bad karma. I kept hitting fast forward and the timeline leapt forward. Oh, the pain of his sister dying wracked through my body until I vomited. Oh, my God! Then I saw it, the moment of Liam's death. He did not look much older than he was now. He was pinned under a boulder. I felt his death moment and there was calm acceptance. At least there was this. I did not want to see any more but I could not stop the visions.

When the Bear came next, I heard a voice in my head, "When the Bear comes, make your way back to the spa. I'm here at what we call '*The Golden Hour.*'"

So I waved the Bear away. I was vaguely aware that I could get more honey down in the Spa. The stairways that led down from each floor were open and always accessible, as opposed to the ones that led up. How many days had it been? I had even lost track of the "Honey Journeys." My body was considerably weaker but I made it down to the spa level one floor below. Walked right through the change room and began to look for Heinz. Luckily, he was right where I saw him last.

"Hmmm," he said as he looked up at me. "Come and sit beside me."

Ohhh, the warm water felt good. I'd almost forgotten how good it had felt, as it seemed like lifetimes since I'd been here last.

"It's good to see you. I was a bit worried about you when you didn't return to the Spa."

"How long have I been away?"

"Over ten 'honey hours,' which is about five days by your reckoning."

"I thought that with all this spiritual development and non-attachment, you wouldn't care if I turned up or not."

"Oh, yes, this happens on the upper levels, but there are always two branches on any path, including the paths here."

"What are the branches?"

"One is Dry and the other is Wet.

"The dryer is more of a solo path and it relies mainly on the mind to bring you to enlightenment. It is what the Tibetans have mapped out so well. Their minds are trained though visualization and meditation to be pristine, and they have created on the topmost floor something they call Dewa Chen--the Pure Land--a place of eternal contentment. The place of fully realized beings. Realized in the sense that they are totally one with the Void and have transcended Samsara and cause and effect. Once you enter Dewa Chen, you do not return."

Dewa Chen and the Heart of a Bodhisattva

"Wow, there *is* a place like that here! I'm not so sure I want to go there. What about the Wet path?"

"On the Wet path we do not enter Dewa Chen. We are connected to the suffering of others, and that is a form of attachment, so we keep returning to alleviate suffering--even though it's an endless task. On the Wet path our ideal is to be a bodhisattva."

I desperately reached around for my small bag of sacred possessions. I had carried it with me through all of this. I was so relieved. I pulled out my large locket and slowly turned the screw handle till it opened. There was a picture of Grandsy and one single pearl. She was a master on the Wet path. As Lama Riksal had said, Grandsy was a returning Bodhisattva. She rose up out of the swirling mist of the pool. I looked over at Heinz and he nodded at me. He could see her, too! How could Grandsy do this? I started weeping as I realized that she had been with me all the time, on my journey through many lifetimes. On our outings, she'd say, "We'll always be together. I will love you always." I felt it was just wishful thinking but now I realize it was literally true. The heart of a Bodhisattva can do this. Travel with you anywhere, forever.

Through the mist, I heard Grandsy's voice: "You must not go to Dewa Chen. In the future, you are meant to have a child whose name is Jo Jo; you must return for Jo Jo."

"A child!" I cried out.

Then the image of Grandsy returned to the mist, and she was gone.

I turned to Heinz, "I must leave this *beyul.*"

"Are you sure? There is so much to learn here. There are twelve more floors to explore. Each represents a chakra and a stage of enlightenment. On the upper floors there are music and art works so sublime you could spend lifetimes exploring. Then there are the libraries and manuscript rooms that hold all the secret teachings from time immemorial. These are all to give you fuel for your inner quest. You may never come across this place again in many lifetimes. It's only one lifetime to give up for the greatest exploration of all time. There are vast hidden worlds here for you to explore."

The Bear returned yet again, and I forgot my desire to return. I made a point to get to the Spa before every Honey Hour. Mostly I made it. I learned to eat more honey and so I did not lose as much weight. From time to time, the Snow Leopard visited me and looked me in the eye and took me up a floor. The raccoons were the ones with the keys to go up. Yes, there was music and art and manuscripts, each appropriate to the floor and to assist you at your stage on the journey. But each floor was also a trap. You could be lulled into that form of pleasure, or locked into a mode of thinking, or an idea that would trap you. And at each floor, your ego was lurking. It was the trickiest of all the creatures here. We visualized it in a hundred ways to force it from the shadows into the open, and yet, there it was, on another floor in another disguise. On the fourth floor, I recognized the ego as fear. Now I knew I was hunting fear and that even the ego was a disguise for fear.

I met others. The *tantrikas* were the most interesting. I realized that they did not need the raccoons to move between floors; they were as at home in the Spa / root chakra as they were in the void near the crown. They moved fluidly. Between what I learned from Heinz and my own explorations I discovered the hidden structure of this place that is known primarily as a *Kabum*. It is a cathedral within the rock. It is one of at least seven. Its hidden name is Bon Core, after the Bon shamans who predated the Buddhists by, according to Heinz, 16,000 years. It has thirteen tapering steps to enlightenment, just like all Buddhist stupas. The large room at the bottom was of course the Spa, and each floor had meditation rooms, galleries of sacred art, music and manuscript rooms. If you looked at it as a three-dimensional floor plan, it was the shape of a mountain inside the stone, with the top single room being the summit. The main stairway spiralled up the centre of it like a spine.

I got a sense that it somehow mirrored the sacred Mountain that Devi and Marie-Madeleine were on their way to--Mt. Kailash. The entire place was designed as a path to awareness and awakening. It was place where time had little or no significance--it was a land of immortals.

Mostly I was content; often I was in awe of how profound a place Bon Core was. Sometimes my longing for the previous life flashed by, but not as often. This was my real life now.

Each floor is a chapter of a book that I may never write. Stories fly by and are dissolved into the vast vault of the never-ending void. Meaninglessness hunts you like a ravenous dog, you feed it a few scraps and it becomes your friend till it grows hungry again. Everything is a dream dreaming itself. There is no solid ground. It is both the pathless way and the way of infinite paths.

From time to time, I became curious as to when and who built and maintained this place. But each time this curiosity grew it seemed that some bigger mind distracted me from this train of thought. I befriended a Tantrika who taught me kundalini yoga as we travelled up and down the spine like a staircase. That way, once I snuck into the manuscript room and discovered that once the creators of this place had formed an alliance with Genghis Khan and that is how many forms of Buddhism spread outside of India and Tibet. It was a failed worldwide spiritual coup they had planned. So Heinrich Himmler, the leader of the Nazi SS, sent Ernst Schäfer to coax the Tibetans to give up their secrets in 1938–39, to further the Nazi goal to attain "perfect spiritual insight and tranquility." They remembered to say no, even though the Nazis offered them power and world spiritual domination . . . perhaps saving the world by doing so.

What I discovered was the Tibetan, Bon and Buddhist devotion to sacred texts and record keeping. What scholars. But more than that, they were devoted to remembering through vast sweeps of time. They measure time in *Kalpas*, which are 16,798,000 years. They knew about these eons of time while much of the Christian West thought the world was 4,000 years old. They learned to hurdle over lifetimes as *tulkus*; through reincarnation, lineages, and manuscripts. Through it all, they saw the impermanence, in both the landscape and in human existence, and learned to swim in it. I was in a shrine, a temple devoted to remembering through time.

And yet I was forgetting to live in this lifetime.

Despite the honey, the Spa, and the stairs keeping my body relatively healthy, I needed sunlight. Kim, one of the *tantrikas*, took me to a higher floor, supposedly the only one close enough to the cliff face where there was an opening--one little window into this vast sandstone cathedral. Together we would meditate in front of the window. I learned that routine, especially here, was important. So, for a couple of hours a day, Kim would practice the six yogas of Naropa, and I would meditate in the sunlight in front of the sky door.

I asked why Heinz had not told me about the sky door. He said that once he had told an adept too soon, and she thought that she could just fly like a bird from the doorway. He said that's one way to leave this place. I asked what the other was.

He replied, "The Reliquary Level, the lowest level, below the Spa."

"What's in the Reliquary Room?" I asked.

"It houses the bones and sacred relics of enlightened beings and

Lamas of high achievement."

Lost and Found

One day I looked back on my life before this place and it seemed like a grain of sand on the beach of time. Little did I know that this single grain of sand was an irritant that created a pearl. While I was meditating in front of the Sky Door, Grandsy's pearls just fell out of my sacred pouch. Each bead came to life and became a wrathful deity. In the midst of this visualization, Rai the Honey Hunter appeared. He insisted that I could use the double *vajras* on the locket he gave me to break through illusions. So I took out my spiritual tools, put Grandsy's pearls on, took out Grandsy's photo, held up the *phurba* (knife), and held the locket with the double *vajras*. Each of the pearls manifested into wrathful deities, and I saw a Kali-like figure cutting through all the worlds of human illusions we have created.

At that moment, I saw that nothing I did in this dream affected anything or anyone. Nothing I did rippled out through this realm of suffering and samsara and touched anyone else. It was all an illusion--an oftentimes beautiful illusion, but still an illusion. It was a virtual world that affected no one else.

It was like instant withdrawal. I saw my own body go through every stage of decomposition, I felt and saw a thousand deaths flash by till I clawed at my own skin and tried to scratch my eyes out. I ran for the doorway, and someone who I thought was Rai could not hold me back from jumping. But at that moment I was hit by hundreds of bees and it was the stingers that woke me from my dream. I opened my eyes and saw that I was in a long-abandoned cave. And through the pain I saw clearly it was Rai, my namesake.

Rai had disturbed the hive by climbing down the cliff; he also was stung many times. The stings were like fire, but we were both now wide-awake. The only way to escape the bees was to run into the cave. I knew every inch of the path, but every room was long since abandoned, looted, and covered in dust. The beams were collapsing and the doors were rotted open. Fortunately, Rai had a flashlight, as the caves were now completely dark. I knew the Snow Leopards were still guarding this place, as I could see the large paw prints everywhere.

We headed up the spiral staircase past all the rooms that I did not get to visit--right to the very summit, the Crown Room. The door was solid, and a light was glowing from under the door. Slowly I opened it and I was hit by a moment of déjà vu. How could I have been here before? The room was lit by butter candles, and there, at the end of the room, as I knew there would be, was an alcove with a bed in it. I saw that there was the form of a very old man under the blankets. His eyes opened; they were the palest blue possible.

"Perhaps you don't recognize me. I am Heinz. I've waited for you."

"How could it all be true?" I asked.

"That is a story for you to tell," Heinz said.

"Please tell us how to get out of here."

"Of course, I've been waiting to tell you."

"How to get past the final trap, right?"

"Right. Did you see the bell on the table outside the Spa?"

"Yes, I noticed it there, despite all the ruin around; I was surprised to see it there."

"Good for you . . . but you still have much to learn."

"You cannot go up to get out, the boulder is still there, and moss has grown over the entrance."

"Over there," he pointed to a small highly decorated door. "This is a door in the sky that leads to the Holy Mountain."

How can that be? Mount Kailash is over fifty miles away.

"You have no time for the answer to that question, and the one to explain it, your Einstein, is on the other side. So you must make up your mind. Do you continue your quest to find Fa and meet your friends at the Holy Mountain or do you return to your Grandsy?"

I thought this over for a few moments,

"Will Shambhala and the Sacred Mountain still be here in a year or two?"

It sounded like a silly question--they had been around for many thousands of years.

But still, Heinz's answer surprised me.

"Shambhala and the Holy Mountain are wherever there is love. Follow love and you will enter the hidden kingdoms of this world; without love, they turn to dust and always elude you."

"Grandsy needs me right now."

"Then she is your doorway to the hidden realms. Never forget that often the way down is the way out. You don't have much time. This particular *beyul* is closing. Go down to the Spa level and ring the bell."

"What about you?"

"Now I can go on my next adventure."

"One more question? Before you were Heinz, who were you?"

"King Suchandra, the first King of Gyanganj, or what you call Shambhala."

"Then you know the secret teaching of Gautama Buddha, the Kalachakra?"

"Yes, I was there for that teaching. And I have been following you for many lifetimes--as you are a *Tulku*. The seeds for this Quest were planted in you many lifetimes ago, and the winds of karma direct your path. So go now and trust that you are a vital part of the Great Perfection."

I kissed Heinz goodbye, and for a moment I saw a king, I saw Fa, I saw all those who were devoted to the light across these small intervals of a single lifetime . . . and somehow a little piece of my heart was made whole.

CHAPTER SIX
THE ANSWER TO THE QUEST

Escape from Paradise

Rai and I made haste back through the door and down stair after stair, right to the landing at the Spa level. We could hear the roar of the snow leopards and hear them coming down the stairs. I rang the bell quickly. For a moment, nothing happened; then an old woman came out from behind the wall.

"English?" she asked.

"Yes," I smiled.

"What can I do for you?"

"Tashi, is there another way out?"

"Of course, there's always a way out."

She motioned for us to follow her behind the wall and pointed us to a hole in the floor.

"This leads to the mortuary (reliquary) room. Cross over the bones and you will see another door. Follow this one and it will take you down to the river. From there, you will know what to do."

"What about you?"

"There is one more person; after that perhaps I will go . . . No time to sit. I will see you again."

"Really?" As I glanced backward, I caught a glimpse of Chokyi smiling.

Still no time to figure this one out.

It was a smooth stone slide down to the reliquary level. We landed in a pile of dusty, unsorted bones. Quite a racket it made. We ran down a long corridor that had alcoves inside where bones were kept alongside sacred instruments and exquisite murals depicting the lives of the high Lamas. After all these years, it had remained hidden and unlooted. There were obviously strong protectors of this place.

I looked over at Rai. I could see that he was tempted to take some of the gemstones but I told him that would be unwise. The power in this room was palpable.

We had almost reached the end of the corridor when, with the greatest of ease, a big snow leopard rounded the corner and strode toward us. There was no sense running. We froze in our spots. The snow leopard, muscles rippling, just ambled on past us. When it was even with me, it looked up and I once again met those blue-green gemstone eyes; I'm pretty sure I saw a smile crease his black lips as he continued past us up the corridor. The exit was directly in front of us.

It was locked, but a moment later, we heard some scrambling and what sounded like complaining. It was an old raccoon, the one I called "Dashi" because he was always scurrying about opening doors. He limped out carrying the big ring of keys, winked at me, and opened the door. I winked back, and together Rai and I entered the dark and dank stairway below Bon Core. As we descended farther, the roar became louder and the walls started to vibrate. We could feel the immense power of water nearby.

I simply had to know. "Rai," I shouted, "how did you know to come looking for me?"

Rai shouted back, "News spread fast through the Gurung villages that a girl had asked to be taken to God's House. I just knew that must be you. So I went to the village. No one would give me any information, as they never talk about who goes to "God's House." I climbed the cliff face and met the Old Man. He had recovered and was meditating in his cave. He described you in detail and told me where you were. I went back to the village and borrowed some rope ladders that we use for Honey Hunting and entered the way the Old Man had told me.

"Or, let's just say I put a GPS in your amulet."

"Right now I'm open to believing anything."

"Are you open to believing I love you?"

I stopped climbing down the stairs and turned and looked up into Rai's eyes and said, "Yes."

Then I started climbing down again.

"Yes--that's it?"

"Yes, and thanks for the amulet; it came in very handy. Look, Rai, for me to say more right now would not be good. I have just lived many lifetimes, I've had four children with you and, to be honest, with others. I have seen my previous and my next lives, I've even seen the deaths of loved ones. So until I sort some of this out, 'Yes' will have to suffice."

"Suffice" seemed like a good word for this moment.

"Okay, 'Yes' will suffice for now."

That was a good place to end the conversation, as the roar and vibration of the walls was extreme, and we were unable to communicate.

The steps were now not sandstone but bedrock and very slick. As we turned a corner, the stairway flattened out and became a tunnel carved out of solid rock. The roar and vibration were directly above us, and water was pouring through the walls. At one point, for a short section we actually had to swim under a submerged part of the tunnel. We came up into a huge cavern. At one end of the cavern there was light flowing in.

We both stood there with our mouths open and gawked.

The opening to the cavern was behind a gigantic waterfall. It was the coolest room ever, but you couldn't stay there long, because of the pounding sound of water. The question of how to escape from under this mammoth volume of water was quickly answered. There was a boat--or more like a raft. Large yak skins had been sewn up and inflated and then ropes fastened to them were attached to a hewn wooden frame. Each yak was head to tail and alongside the next yak, so the underside of the raft looked like a tight herd of yaks five across and three wide. There were some paints stored nearby and so we began to decorate our boat. We called it "Yak Attack."

While the paint was drying, I began to get hungry. Rai had brought some *tsampa* balls. I shouted in his ear, "Is there any *raksi* in them?" Rai looked at me a bit strangely. Then I noticed there in the cavern were what looked like honey baskets. I opened one of the old lids. I was amazed at how long honey lasts. I was about to dip my *tsampa* balls into the vat, but Rai took my hand in his, shook his head, and held me for a few moments while I had a good cry.

First Descent of God's House

We carried the yak-skin boat to a quiet little pool that flowed down into the roaring chasm just above the base of the waterfall. We tied our possessions to the raft and grabbed a couple of good, stout poles. One end was designed for pushing off; the other, wider end was for paddling.

We both shouted *"Ta do-ran-sha!"* above the roar of the water ("It's time to go!"). We looked at each other, both eager for the adventure--and not surprisingly a little nervous. I shouted, "Bon Core, *Mon Amore!*" And we both pushed away from shore with our poles.

Instantly a ton of water descended on us and our yak-skin boat struggled and bounced up and down trying to shed the water fast enough to stay afloat. Then, when it looked like we were going under, all of a sudden we were weightless and falling with the water. Seconds later, our boat landed just outside of the main flow, and we bounced free of the waterfall.

We both looked back in amazement. The cave we came from was invisible behind the waterfall, and just above our cave, the entire river came out of a huge crack in the solid stone cliff face.

"OH, BOY!" I cried, "from the frying pan to the fire, as Grandfa would say. This means we're just above the rapids called God's House. They're rated as Class five-plus!"

"What's it out of--ten?" asked Rai.

"Five," I replied.

We were just turning a bend in the river.

"OH, BOY!" shouted Rai, pointing ahead.

All I could see were massive haystacks and drops. No doubt this one contained just about every kind of hazard.

I raised my pole in the air and yelled, "Yak Attack!"

Rai raised his pole and shouted, "Yak Attack!"

Then, on the stone beach beside the main section of God's House, I saw Mum and Liam! They were looking right at us with shocked faces, and we just swept right past them. Mum reached out with her hand. But there was no way to get to shore, so we held on to the tumpline straps and Rai yelled, "*Tso Tso!*"

That's what Tibetans cry out when they reach the top of high passes: "Victory to the Gods!"

Out of the corner of my eye I saw Liam race for his kayak, his team following close behind. In one fluid motion, he leapt into his kayak and pushed off, and within seconds he was right behind us as we rode through God's House. Midway through the rapids, we got caught in a giant hole and water was coming down on us as our boat strove to stay afloat. Liam threw Rai and me a rope that Rai lashed to the boat. Putting his kayak sideways to the huge current, Liam generated a lot of force that slowly pulled us free of the hole. After that, the rest of the rapids was a fun ride. As the current lessened, Liam pulled us to shore. I jumped out of the raft and gave him the biggest hug. Mum was running down the beach and jumped right on top of the three of us, so un-Mum like.

I introduced Mum and Liam to Rai. There was the whole business of, "Haven't we met before?" as they remembered each other from the stupa in Kathmandu. As they got to know each other, I just fell onto the sand and looked up at the sky and watched the clouds float from east to west I remembered a piece of text that I'd read in one of the manuscript rooms:

Just as a white summer-cloud, in harmony with heaven and earth, freely floats in the blue sky from horizon to horizon, following the breath of the atmosphere--in the same way the pilgrim abandons himself to the breath of the greater life that wells up from the depth of his being and leads him beyond the farthest horizons to an aim which is already present within him, though yet hidden from his sight. Lama Govinda--The Way of the White Cloud

Finding the Answer Within

The rest of the trip, I just floated through. I hung out with Rai and we got to know each other better. Mum was more relaxed than I'd ever seen her--while still being Mum, of course. Liam and his team were awesome. They entertained us on the water and on land. When they finished getting the footage they needed for their film, we all floated down to Simikot, which was the takeout spot for the expedition. After what I'd seen happen to Liam at Bon Core, I was relieved that we had all reached the end of the kayaking expedition safely.

Rai and I were in a small way famous. It turned out that Liam's team was just setting up to run the Upper God's House rapids when we swept by on our yak-skin boat, and so we scooped the first descent, which over the years became a story in itself.

Mum so loved the sacred music in Nepal that she picked up some Tibetan Singing Bowls in Kathmandu and has been offering sound healing sessions in Mt. Albert.

I still have the locket, and next year Rai plans to visit Canada. In the meantime, I continue to wear the *bindi* he put on my forehead.

Some of you might want to know if I brought a pet back with me. I have a habit of getting attached to animals and then bending the rules a bit--my dear little meerkat being a precious example. Not this time, but guess what! When we were camped along the Karnali, a large-eared pika must have crawled into the bottom of my backpack. And believe you me, there are enough crumbs down there to live on for a year. Thank goodness Lufthansa has pressurized luggage compartments and so you can imagine my surprise when I heard scratching as I lifted my backpack from the airport limo. It seems the little pika was just as happy to see me.

While in Nepal and hearing Lama's Riksal teaching on *naga teeth*, I realized that River never had told me the story of Fa's first and most perfect river tooth. So on the last days of the holiday I decided to return to Minden with Liam to tell River about *naga teeth* and hear about Fa's first river tooth. While waiting on the bridge just above the Minden White Water Preserve, I thought about mischief, Mum's pink bathing suit, and how the most seemingly small things can lead to such remarkable events.

It was the butterfly effect. Before long, I spotted River in his old truck and hailed him down.

"Is that Ray with an E or a Y?" River hollered.

"With a Y! Is that the River that runs wild and free?"

"Not if my old truck gets her way. She'll have me stocking shelves in the local Foodland."

"Maybe we'll both work there next summer," I added.

"Maybe," said River. "Now don't tell me you came all this way to shoot the breeze with an old man."

"Well, as a matter of fact I did. You never told me how Fa came across his first river tooth."

"Oh, there's not much to it, as I remember. Your Fa was heading down to some kind of storytelling workshop in Colorado or Utah and he was looking through various bags for an object to take with him and function as a storytelling stick. He reached into a backpack he hadn't used in four or five years.

"Now, as I recall, your Fa had heard about river teeth in a Quarterly literary magazine that was called *River Tooth*. In it, they gave a short description of a river tooth, and from that moment on, your Fa looked along many rivers but never found one.

"So, five years later, your Fa was reaching into his backpack, and from a small pocket he pulled out this wooden object. It was shaped like a perfect human tooth but much larger. That's when he recognized it was his first river tooth--and he had had it all along. Even before he read about them or knew what they were. Fancy that."

"Where did he originally find that river tooth?"

"The Kettle Valley in British Columbia. Your Fa and I went there together, but that's another story you must come back for."

"I promise I will."

On the bus back, I got to pondering the poem "Little Gedding" by T.S. Eliot.

Through the unknown, unremembered gate
When the last of earth left to discover
Is that which was the beginning;
At the source of the longest river
The voice of the hidden waterfall
And the children in the apple-tree . . .
. . . We shall not cease from exploration
And the end of all our exploring
Will be to arrive where we started
And know the place for the first time.

So: Did I return to Mt. Albert and start high school at the end of the summer? No, I did not. I came to live with Grandsy and went to my first year of high school at Riverdale High, just around the corner from Grandsy's house. Most weekends I went back to Mt. Albert, but just as often, Mum came to visit Grandsy. It was like having a house in the country and one in the city.

Grandsy was so excited to see me back and even more excited to hear that I was coming to live with her. I reluctantly gave Grandsy her pearls back.

"I knew those pearls would bring you back safely. Did you find Shambhala, dear?" Grandsy asked.

"Yes, I did."

"Well, let's have a cup of tea and some sherry and you can tell me all about it."

"You cannot stay on the summit forever; you have to come down again. So why bother in the first place? Just this: What is above knows what is below, but what is below does not know what is above. One climbs, one sees. One descends, one sees no longer, but one has seen. There is an art of conducting oneself in the lower regions by the memory of what one saw higher up. When one can no longer see, one can at least still know."

Rene Dumal--Mt. Analogue.

ABOUT THE AUTHOR

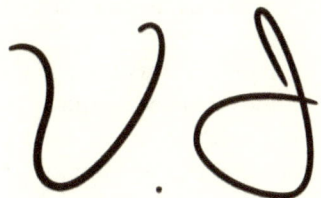

Verity can often be found writing outdoors in a tent where the walls are thin; participating in the great tide of nature, coyotes howling, driving rain, snow storms, great gusts of wind, geese flying northward, even the occasional opossum lumbering on by.

I have chosen to write under my Grandmother's surname, which is Verity, meaning, "a true principle or belief, especially one of fundamental importance." I am one of a long line of seekers of truth and I hope some of these "truths" have resonated with you.

Please join Ray and myself on our other life-affirming adventures.

Other stories in the series:

Ray 1: Quest for the First Hive
Ray 2: The Butterfly Bard

If you have read all three novels then email me at verity@verityjenkins.com and I will send you a short novella that is not available anywhere else.

Also consider: *The Ray Adventure Series Omnibus* that is available in ebook, pint and a collector's hardcover edition.

Please go to www.verityjenkins.com to purchase from all major booksellers and to join the Ray Change Agent community and gain access to a Ray Storytelling online program.

Ray Origin Story

Ray is the very tip of a mighty spear that pierces time.

Each one of us, whether we know it or not, is the sharpened head of an arrow that has flown through eons. We see this speck of life we inhabit and don't know that encoded within us is the entire journey of the time-traveling projectile that brought us here.

Our culture does not contain the mythology that allows us to inhabit these broader reaches of time. Yet occasionally we catch glimpses of something much older within ourselves.

My brother David Jenkins, is a medical doctor, my father John Jenkins was a surgeon, his father was a priest, his father was a local General Practitioner in Wales and before that a priest. And so on as far back as our family history goes, doctor, priest, doctor, priest. Like turtles all the way down. What accounts for this pattern?

One day it just became obvious. One thousand years ago on my father's side we were the Druids, the doctor/priests of the ancient Celts, and that pattern has remained written into some part of my nature, and each of my ancestors nature, that hides behind free will.

The Druids were not only the doctors and the priests, they were also the storytellers. It was the bardic portion of what was called the "triple gift." It involved nineteen rigorous years of training to develop. They not only knew plant medicine and were the healers, but they also doctored, steered & maintained the Celtic society as Bards.

Is it possible that I, Verity Jenkins, am the very tip of the spear that traveled through time from the ancients to NOW? Is it possible that you are as well?

What am I carrying that has survived such a long journey? I am carrying Ray. She is the daughter I never had. A modern-day Druidic Priestess in training. Ray's desire to heal the world and be a storyteller has ancient roots. Although she's mischievous and playful, her altruistic nature propels her on adventure after adventure. In her own words, "The world will just not stay saved."

Over and over, since the beginning of human history, heroes like Ray have redeemed the world from our darker nature. What keeps Ray and myself heading towards the light is the altruistic quest, the bardic gift, the wisdom of our ancestors and the wonders of nature.

To the Ray in you,

Verity Jenkins
Whitestone, Ontario

Dear Ray Reader, what's next?

You are at the end of Book 3 in this series. Thanks for joining Ray on this journey to discover how we can bring each other back to life. I hope this story was an inspiration to you and you resonated with the messages.

I have a number of other novels in the works, but in the meantime please enjoy a Ray Novella called Saved! - if you've not already read it. It's free. I'll include a sample at the end of this book but you can download it for any device here – and sign up for our monthly newsletter.
https://www.verityjenkins.com/saved

To find out more, here's a link to the Ray Change Agent website. It's my hope that you will sign up for the newsletter and become part of the Ray Team.
https://www.verityjenkins.com

On the site you can access a free *StoryAwake* course that helps storytellers in training to be *Change Agents*. By sharing your story and what you care about - you can change the world.
https://www.verityjenkins.com/storytelling

The author has a patron page for those who support the Ray Vision and wish to help other's change the world by telling Better Stories. If you liked these messages and would consider donating, here's the link:
https://www.verityjenkins.com/support-the-vision

If you want to ask me a question or just drop me a note then here's my email address: verity@verityjenkins.com
Anything else can be found here: https://www.verityjenkins.com/

I hope this story has awoken the Ray in you,

Verity Jenkins

Following this enjoy a sample of the FREE Ray Novella Saved!

THERE'S A RAT IN MY BURGER

The Edge of a Funk

It's four days before Christmas. Mum has decided not to get a tree this year. She doesn't like the idea of millions of people cutting down trees; and of course the plastic ones are just plain cheesy.

She asks, "Why can't we imagine the pine in our backyard as our Christmas tree?"

"Really, Mum! Next we'll be imagining presents. Christmas is already NOT my favourite time of year, and now you're making it worse."

I'm full of so many thousands of images of how Christmas should be; so when it's not like in the ads, I feel ripped off; or, at the very least, I feel some vague, unspecific anxiety that my life is already a failure.

Then I saw it--it happened in slow motion. I was in Mount Albert at the Mad Hatter's Café (it used to be called the Banana Bread Café), sitting at the window, gazing and sipping a chai latte. The Indian spices, the black tea, the warm milk and honey were just beginning to realign my brain chemistry, and I was slipping into bliss. When down the hill, through the small town, right in front of the window rolled a long tractor-trailer. A massive, juicy, beautifully garnished, perfect in every way hamburger rolled by at eye level, not more than ten feet away. I was mesmerized.

Now, I'm a loveatarian (a kind of vegetarian). I don't eat animals that love, because I know what it's like to lose someone you love--and I know cows love. I lived right across from a farm and when a young calf is taken from its mother--as is a common practice--both the mother and her calf bellow in the most heartbreaking way for nearly a week! So I know they love. Nobody could hear that and not recognize it.

But now my mouth was watering for a big, juicy hamburger, and at the very least Mum and I had to go to Licks for a Nature Burger--immediately! Otherwise, I would certainly get an ulcer from all the gastric juices cascading into my meagre latte.

Mum was not answering! I forced myself to sit and try to enjoy my latte and recover my senses. Then a thought came to me.

Maybe all these messages are making me dissatisfied, maybe I was being manipulated by them?

Perhaps deception is so commonplace, so bold, so in your face, that you do not see it.

And does a Big Mac really look like this? Does it ever look this perfect? And, it is so way out of proportion! It's like a tall tale, a great edible exaggeration.

I have to admit that I exaggerate a bit, too. What storyteller doesn't?

Take Alice in Wonderland: everything is larger or smaller than it seems. Alice is either too big to fit, or too small to do anything. Nothing seems to be right sized.

Last week, I was listening to Aunt Thelma tell stories. She told us that she'd driven a golf cart up a tree; another time, she hit a tree so hard with the golf cart, she knocked ALL the bark off it! Then, when she took driver's training, she drove down the ditch and accelerated up the other side onto someone's lawn and tore up all the grass, which needed reseeding. The Drivers Training Company had to pay for it--after all, as Aunt Thelma maintained, "They have insurance for just that sort of thing."

To storytellers, things are not as they appear. It's like we give the storyteller permission to bring out the details in such a way that brings us a more interesting story. It's an age-old deal between the storyteller and the listener.

Are the new storytellers marketers? The storytellers that used to be the elders and the medicine people, the dreamers, the poets, the painters and the mystics--have we lost these storytellers from the helm of our culture? Are marketers at the helm of culture now, taking advantage of this age-old deal?

The question: Is a burger just a burger? Or is it an icon, a symbol for much more? For our lifestyle, our diet, for our planetary report card, for our humanity--is it one of the chains of deception that I can follow?

Fa told me a story about hamburgers that's an entirely random prank, but I like it partly because it has no point, and partly because Mum didn't.

Fa's hockey team was being slaughtered out on the ice on a regular basis. They had boldly gotten their little welfare community of Boyle Street, which previously had no hockey team, voted into the Edmonton Hockey League. There had been no new teams in twenty years, so it was a big accomplishment for them. Fa's Mum had got Furniture Place to become a team sponsor. They paid for brand-new jerseys with a custom logo, and the Edmonton Oilers farm team donated their used goalie equipment.

Their first game on the ice, Fa's team lost 40–1 in front of a record crowd. (Forty, that's like basketball.) The other team accidentally scored one goal--on their own net. So you can imagine their spirits were pretty low after most games. According to Fa, the team improved (there's nowhere to go but up from there), even winning some games near the end of the season.

That year, they won the league trophy for "The Team with the Most Desire to Win." Which to my mind is a very questionable award.

But anyway, after the game, defeated in spirit, Fa would think up a little escapade to cheer the team up. This particular Saturday, Fa announced that during their outing to McDonalds, each person had to follow these instructions to the letter:

Everyone was to change out of their team sweater.

No one was to know that they were all together.

In pairs they would enter McDonalds over a period of fifteen minutes.

They were to sit together in pairs.

Each person was to order two Big Macs, eat one, and take exactly one bite of the second Big Mac.

After that, they were to wait and do exactly what Fa did.

They were generally a dispirited group, so they just went along with Fa's plans. It was a relatively busy Saturday afternoon when the team entered McDonalds. Each person ordered two Big Macs and sat down with their teammate. There was no crosstalk.

Fa teamed up with the person that needed the most encouragement. After ordering their Big Macs and sitting down, Fa ate one of the Big Macs and then took one single bite of his second Big Mac. Fa then reminded his teammate to do exactly what he did, move for move, and say exactly what he said, word for word. Nervously his teammate, Robbie shook his head in agreement.

Then Fa stood up, with his burger in hand, stepped up on to the chair and waited silently, until most people in the restaurant were watching. Then Fa stepped up onto the table and waited a few more moments. Now almost no one was moving and everyone's eyes were on Fa. At that moment he opened up the bun on his Big Mac and shouted,

"There's a rat in my burger!"

Then he brought both halves back together and, winding up, pitched a no-hitter right across the restaurant toward the counter. It sailed over people's heads across the counter and in toward the industrial kitchen.

Splat! Went that special sauce and factory-farmed, rainforest beef against some stainless steel machine.

No one moved.

Fa climbed down slowly and gave his partner a look that said now or never. Robbie ascended the chair and stepped up onto the table like a zombie.

His face was white as a sheet but he still he opened up his Big Mac and managed to croak out, "There's a rat in my burger."

Then he gave it a half-hearted throw toward the counter. His Big Mac hit another person, who just happened to be on our team, and who was about to blow it by blasting Robbie with his Big Mac, when another team-member in another section climbed onto the table and shouted,

"There's a rat in my burger, too!"

And heaved it toward the counter, dinging one of the McDonalds serving staff.

Now the hockey team was popping up all over the restaurant, shouting, "There's a rat in my burger!" and flinging their burgers toward the counter.

Sixteen people in the space of one or two minutes uttered the word "rat" and "burger." The air was thick with patties, secret sauce, lettuce, and buns. Sporadically, like machine-gun fire, you could hear that quite particular saucy thwack that Big Macs make.

The staff were ducking and running for cover. It was like a war zone behind the counter. However, two or three of the short-order cooks rose to the occasion, and, armed with a dozen or so Big Macs, were staging a counterattack, most of them hitting other patrons. This was a bit of a surprise for the team, but not an unwelcome one. What did amaze Fa was that two or three people that Fa did not recognize stood up on their tables and shouted, "There's a rat in my burger!" and joined the attack. So there is something about rats and burgers that is in the collective unconscious.

In pairs, the team beat a hasty escape while the mayhem was still in full swing. The team did not return to that particular McDonalds for nearly six months.

Maybe it was in my blood to pull pranks like Fa. But a prank like this is too random for me. It needs to be more connected to a quest, something meaningful. Something more like collective action.

END OF FIRST CHAPTER OF SAVED!

To find out more and get Saved! As a free gift….

Visit: https://www.verityjenkins.com/saved

Please review this book!

Reviews help authors more than you might think. If you enjoyed *Shambhala* please consider leaving a review on the website of the bookseller you purchased this book from and also on Goodreads – it would be greatly appreciated by me.

Say Hello!

You can connect with me in a number of places. I am committed to supporting readers telling their story and developing an active community of change agents. If you have a story you wish to tell then reach out to: verity@verityjenkins.com & on the website at www.verityjenkins.com as there is so much more to explore.

www.ingramcontent.com/pod-product-compliance
Lightning Source LLC
Chambersburg PA
CBHW030617130626
46552CB00002B/606